NEW YO

CHERIE
BRADSHAW

BELLE MANOR
HAUNTING

This book is a work of fiction. Names, characters, places, businesses, and incidents either are the products of the author's imagination or are used in a fictitious manner. Any similarity to events or locales or persons, living or dead, is entirely coincidental.

First US edition February 2020
Copyright © 2020 by Cheryl Bradshaw
Cover Design Copyright 2020 © Indie Designz
All rights reserved.
ISBN: 9798604171240

"A child is a person who is going to carry on what you have started ... the fate of humanity is in his hands."

—Abraham Lincoln

CHAPTER 1

Addison Lockhart was holding a jar of tomato sauce in her hand when her water broke. She'd been shopping at the local grocery store when her unborn child decided she'd grown a bit tired of sitting inside of a stuffy womb for so many months. She was ready to make her grand entrance into the world, even if it was nine days ahead of schedule.

Shocked and unprepared, Addison stood for a moment, frozen, staring down at the combination of tomato sauce, glass, and amniotic fluid that had splattered all over the supermarket floor.

A young male employee stepped into the aisle, glancing at the mess as if confused about what to do next.

He looked at Addison and said, "Ma'am, are you all right?"

She stared at him and then tipped her head toward the wet patch on her dress. "I don't think so. It seems my baby's coming."

The employee's eyes widened, and he held his hands in front of him. "I … ahh … you just wait here. I'll get someone to help."

He scampered off, and moments later, a voice came over the store's intercom requesting a cleanup on aisle three. Addison reached down, attempting and failing to grab her purse at the bottom of the shopping cart before a sharp pain ripped across her abdomen. She gripped the cart's handle in her trembling hands, trying her best to breathe through it.

I can do this. It's just a contraction. All I need to do is breathe through it, and everything will be all right.

If only she believed it.

A bit farther down the aisle, an elderly woman rushed to Addison's side. The woman leaned over the cart, lifting the purse like it weighed nothing. She handed the bag to Addison and said, "Here you go, hun."

Addison forced a smile. "Thanks for your help." Then she unzipped the top of her purse, fumbled around for her cell phone, pressed the first number on her speed dial, and waited for the call to go through.

Seconds later, Luke answered, saying, "I was just getting ready to call you. Want to grab lunch somewhere?"

"I think I'm in labor. My water just broke."

"Already? Where are you?"

"I'm at Fresh Pantry, the one by our place."

"I'm on my way. I'll be there in five minutes."

Addison ended the call, slid the phone back inside her purse, and slung the purse over her shoulder. She glanced over to see the elderly woman still standing by her side, smiling.

"Is this your first baby?" the woman asked.

"It is."

The woman reached out, patting Addison's hand. "Now, don't you worry. Everything is going to work out. How about I walk you to the front door and wait with you until your ride gets here?"

"I appreciate your help. I think I can make it."

Addison abandoned the cart and started walking toward the end of the aisle. Several steps in, another wave of contractions began. Addison bent down and reached out, clutching the shelf next to her.

The woman wrapped an arm around her and said, "Let's get you through this one, and I'll help you get where you need to be. Okay?"

Addison nodded.

The woman remained by Addison's side, humming a soothing tune as they made their way to the door. The tune seemed familiar. Addison was sure she'd heard it before—somewhere. She glanced over, giving the woman a closer look. She estimated the woman to be in her eighties, and she had short, gray hair styled into a messy pixie cut. The woman was thin but much stronger than she appeared.

They walked outside, and the woman guided her to a bench. They both sat down. Addison turned toward the woman. "I didn't think my baby was coming yet or I wouldn't have gone to the store today."

"Hard to know with babies, isn't it? They're unpredictable little bundles. You have a name picked out yet?"

Addison nodded. "Amara Jane."

"It's lovely. How did you choose it?"

"It may sound strange, but her name just came to me one day."

Addison thought back to the day of her grandmother's funeral. As she left the graveyard, a breeze had kicked up out of nowhere, and with it, Addison swore she'd heard someone whisper *Amara.* As her pregnancy progressed, Addison and Luke considered several names, but no matter which ones they liked, she always came back to Amara.

"Do you have any children?" Addison asked.

"A daughter, a son, and one granddaughter."

"I'm Addison, by the way. What's your name?"

"Josephine. You can call me Jo."

"Do you live around here?"

"Not far. I always thought I'd move on from this place one day, take a journey, see the world, but I've always found it hard to be away from my children for long."

"My father feels the same way. He just bought the house next door to ours."

"Do you mind him being so close?"

Addison shook her head. "Not at all. I love my husband, but my dad is the only family I have left."

A car raced into the parking lot, not bothering to brake when it hit the speed bump near the store's entrance.

"I'm guessing your ride's here," the woman said.

Addison stood. "It is. Thanks again for looking out for me today. I don't know what I would have done if you weren't there."

"You would have been just fine, but I was happy to help. Maybe one day we'll meet again, and you can return the favor."

Luke jerked the car to a stop next to Addison, hopped out, and rushed around the side. He jerked the passenger-side door open and eyed Addison. Then he placed his hands on her shoulders and squeezed. "How are you doing? Are you okay? I mean, are you all right? Are you in pain? What can I do? I'm here. Just tell me. Tell me what to do, and I'll do it."

Addison grinned. "For starters, you can ease up on your grip a bit and calm down."

"Calm down. Right. Sorry."

He helped her into the car, buckled her into the seat belt, and raced to the driver's seat.

"I know how much you want to hurry," Addison said, "but let's just concentrate on getting there safely, okay?"

Luke had always been the calm, collected type, while Addison had always considered herself to be a bit unsure about things and scattered. Seeing his cork come undone shouldn't have been satisfying, but somehow, it was.

"How are you feeling?" Luke asked.

"I've had a couple of contractions since my water broke. I honestly didn't know what to do, and then this sweet woman offered to help me. She walked me outside and stayed with me until you got here."

"Too bad I didn't get the chance to thank her."

"I'm sorry. I was concentrating so much on getting out of there, I didn't give it much thought. I should have. She was sitting right next to me."

"When?"

"Just now. On the bench when you pulled up."

He shook his head, confused. "Sweetie, I saw you as soon as I drove in. You were alone on the bench. There was no one else with you."

CHAPTER 2

Four hours later Amara Jane entered the world at seven pounds, one ounce. After bundling her tiny frame inside a blanket, the nurse placed her in Addison's arms. Addison stared down into the bright, sparkling eyes of her newborn daughter, feeling a rush of overwhelming joy and love. A kind of love she'd never experienced before—not like this.

Addison reflected on how much had changed in her life over the last few years. Following her mother's death, she'd learned of Grayson Manor, a home she'd inherited in Rhinebeck, New York. It was there she'd first met Luke and reconnected with her grandmother, Marjorie, who had made Addison aware of who she was, and the supernatural power the women in their family possessed.

Addison now understood why her mother had kept her from becoming who she was meant to be all those years ago. She'd tried to protect her, but she hadn't protected her at all. Even as a child, Addison had still experienced visions and saw things she couldn't explain. Looking back on it now, Addison made a promise to herself. She wouldn't allow her own child to suffer as she had. She'd raise her from the start knowing who she was, the power she held, and what she would become.

Luke slipped his hand inside Addison's and bent down, kissing Amara Jane on the forehead. He brushed a wisp of Addison's hair off her face and said, "You look tired. You should get some sleep."

"I know," Addison replied. "All I want to do is hold her in my arms and never let go. I have no idea how I'm going to handle being away from her one day. Is that weird? I mean, she just arrived, and already I can't imagine a day where I have to let her go out on her own in the world."

Luke squeezed Addison's hand. "It's not weird. I understand. I feel … I don't know how to describe it. Having our little one has made our lives so—"

"Complete?" Addison suggested.

He nodded. "Yeah, complete. We're our own family now."

"I have been keeping her all to myself since the nurse handed her off to me. You're right, though. I should get some rest. I know you've waited for your turn with her. Ready to take her?"

Luke nodded and bent down, lifting Amara Jane into his arms. "Looks like she's waking up. Why don't I walk her in the hall for a while?"

Addison nodded. "All right."

Father and daughter left the room. A few minutes later, the door creaked open. Addison opened her eyes and looked over, wondering why Luke had returned so soon. She was surprised to find he wasn't the one who'd entered the room. Standing in front of her was a little girl who looked to be around six years old. Her long, brown hair was in pigtails, and she wore a pink zip-up jacket and matching pink pants. Her arms were clutched around a stained, ratty-looking, brown teddy bear.

The child blinked at Addison and said, "I can't find Scarlett. I think she's lost. She said she'd come back, and she didn't. Do you know where she is?"

Addison sat up. "I'm sorry, sweetie. I don't know Scarlett."

The girl nodded and then burst into tears.

"It's going to be all right," Addison said. "Is Scarlett your sister?"

"She's my nanny. She takes care of me sometimes."

"Why is she in the hospital? Did something happen?"

The girl shrugged. "I don't know. I don't remember. I'm scared."

"You don't have to be scared. I'm sure she's not far. What's your name?"

"Sara."

"I'm Addison."

Sara sniffled and said, "Why are *you* in the hospital? Are you hurt?"

"I just had a baby."

Addison pushed her blanket to the side, wincing in discomfort as she scooted off the bed, and bent down toward Sara. "How about we go find Scarlett together? I bet if we talk to one of the nurses, they'll know where to find her."

Sara shrugged. "Okay, but I talk to them, and they don't talk back."

The comment seemed odd, and when Addison reached a hand out to Sara, she discovered why. Sara took her hand, and the room went black.

CHAPTER 3

Addison glanced around, taking in the strange surroundings. One thing was certain: she was no longer in a hospital room. At present, she was in the back seat of what appeared to be a vintage car. Sara was seated next to her with her arms wrapped around the same teddy bear she'd been holding moments before.

The car's speakers blasted Carly Simon's "You're So Vain" at full volume, and in the front seat, a college-aged boy and girl attempted to sing along. The girl was in the driver's seat, and the boy was next to her, bouncing one of his tan, suede boots on the car's dashboard. The song came to an end, and when the next one began, the girl leaned over and switched the radio off.

The boy glared at her, annoyed. "What did you do that for? I liked that song. It's groovy, baby."

"Yeah, well, I'm tired of it. They play it all the time. I won't be able to get it out of my head for the rest of the day now."

He laughed. "Yeah, well, that's why it's so good, and you're not the only one in the car, you know. Maybe we should put it to a vote."

The girl looked over her shoulder at Sara and said, "What do you think, hun? Do you want the radio on or off?"

Sara thought about it. "I want ice cream."

"Good answer," the boy said. "I want ice cream, too, just as soon as the song is over."

He reached over and turned the radio back on. The girl rolled her eyes, but this time, she gave in to his wishes.

It seemed Addison was in one of Sara's memories. If so, she assumed Sara brought her there for a reason, to show Addison something she wanted her to see.

Addison turned toward Sara. "Where are we? Why have you taken me back to this particular memory?"

Sara didn't respond.

"Sara, can you hear me?" Addison asked. "What is it you want me to see? It's okay. You can tell me. Whatever happened before, you're safe now."

When there was still no reply, Addison tried placing a hand on Sara's shoulder, but her hand swiped right through it.

Sara turned toward Addison, pressed a finger to her own lips, and said, "Shhh. Just wait. We're almost there."

"Wait for what? What's about to happen?"

"You'll see," Sara said.

The boy up front leaned over and kissed the girl on the cheek. "Hey, baby, how about we go to the drive-in and see *American Graffiti* after you put the little one to bed?"

"I can't," the girl said. "Not tonight."

"Why not?"

"Sara's mom went into the city with friends. She won't be back until tomorrow."

"Yeah, so?"

"I'm staying over," the girl said.

The boy frowned, displeased. "Why? Sara's dad will be home to look after her, won't he?"

The girl nodded. "Yeah, he'll be around, but Mr. Belle has friends coming over tonight. I want to be there for Sara in case she needs anything."

Belle.

The name was familiar.

"She'll be sleeping," the boy said. "What could she need?"

"I've already told him I'll stay over, and I'm not going back on it now."

The boy grinned and looked back at Sara like he'd found a solution where everyone got what they wanted. "Hey, kiddo, you wouldn't mind if I borrowed Scarlett tonight for a couple hours after you go to bed, would ya? I'll throw in a second scoop of ice cream to make it worth your while."

Sara's eyes widened with delight, but before she had the chance to reply, Scarlett intercepted.

"Knock it off, Theo. Don't do that."

"Don't do *what*?" Theo asked.

"Use Sara to get what you want. It won't work. I said not tonight, and I meant it."

Theo threw his hands in the air. "What's gotten into you today? You're actin' kinda crazy. What's the skinny?"

Scarlett breathed a heavy sigh. "I've … I'm sorry, Theo. I don't mean to blow you off. It's just, I have a lot on my mind. I've lost something … something important."

"What did you lose?"

"It doesn't matter. I just need to find it."

Theo gave Scarlett's shoulder a squeeze. "All I wanted was to spend some time with my girl. That so bad?"

"You will," Scarlett said. "I'll make it up to you tomorrow night. Mmm…kay?"

Theo leaned back. He folded his arms and huffed like a vexed child. "I mean, I guess so."

"How much longer?" Sara asked. "I'm hungry."

"A few more minutes," Scarlett said. "We're almost there. I just need to make a quick stop for your dad first."

Scarlett turned onto Dawson Street, and Addison gazed out the window. The street was familiar. The surroundings were not. The barren field on the right had been turned into a strip mall in the present day, and the fast-food diner on the left was now a Brazilian Steakhouse.

Addison looked at Scarlett and Theo, studying their clothes. Scarlett was dressed in a white, tie-neck mini dress. Theo was in burgundy bell-bottoms and a striped button-up shirt.

From the looks of things, Addison was locked in a seventies time warp.

Theo jerked his head to the right and shouted, "Scarlett, Look out!"

A truck traveling the opposite direction plowed through the stop sign, slamming into the car Scarlett was driving. The car spun 'round and 'round, skidding across the street, before nose-diving into a tree. When everything came to a sputtering stop and Addison's head stopped spinning, she opened her eyes and canvassed her surroundings. She was seated on the ground several feet from the car. She looked herself up and down. There wasn't a scratch on her.

Her thoughts turned to the car's other passengers.

Addison's eyes first came to rest on Theo. He had been thrown from the vehicle, his bloodied body lying face down on the pavement. Addison stood up and ran toward the car. Scarlett was in the front seat. The smashed-up auto had folded into itself, sandwiching Scarlett between twisted layers of bent metal. Half of the back seat had been ripped off, and Sara was missing. So was the other car and its driver. Apparently, the offender had just driven off.

Addison whipped around and shouted, "Sara! Where are you? Can you hear me?"

Cars screeched to a stop on both sides of the road, taking in the gruesome sight. People leapt from their cars and bolted to the scene of the accident, slapping their hands over their mouths and standing in horror as they witnessed the accident's deadly aftermath.

A small group of people huddled together on the other side of the car. At first, Addison assumed they were discussing what they'd just seen until a teary-eyed woman dropped to the ground. Addison squeezed through the growing group of spectators, fearing the worst. There, on the ground, bruised and broken, was Sara's lifeless body.

CHAPTER 4

"Addison, can you hear me?"

Luke's voice seemed distant like he was calling to her from the opposite end of a long corridor. Her eyes opened, and she found herself on the floor in the hospital room. Luke hovered over her.

Addison sat up, her eyes darting around. "Where did she go? Where is she?"

"Amara Jane? She's with your dad. He's just outside the door. I can get him if you like. I wanted to check on you first before I brought her back to you. I thought you might be asleep."

"I wasn't talking about the baby. I mean …"

Sara. She meant Sara. The present moment didn't seem like the right time to discuss what had occurred over the last several minutes. Luke had been aware of Addison's unique abilities for years, and though he'd always been supportive, once Addison became pregnant, his concern about her afterlife visitors heightened when he thought about what it meant for their baby. Addison didn't choose when a spirit made contact, and she hadn't had any such visits since she first learned she was pregnant. For a while she'd wondered if she'd been given a short reprieve—a reprieve that seemed to be over.

Addison reached for Luke's hand, and she came to a standing position.

"What happened?" Addison asked.

"I hoped you could tell me. I came back into the room and found you on the floor. I was just headed to the nurse's station to get help. I thought you were unconscious."

"How long was I out?"

"I'm not sure. I found you about thirty seconds before your eyes opened. How did you end up on the floor in the first place?"

Addison looked away, unsure of the explanation she wanted to give. She didn't want to lie. She didn't want to tell the truth, either. Not yet.

He raised a brow. "It happened, didn't it? Someone made contact."

Addison nodded. "A little girl named Sara. She came into my room looking for her nanny. I didn't know she wasn't alive at first. She was crying, and she looked scared. I got out of bed, and said I'd help her. I took her hand, and the room went dark. When the darkness cleared, I found myself back in the seventies."

"The seventies?"

"I believe it's the time period Sara died in. I think her parents own Belle Manor, the house in the forest above the city."

"Belle Manor. I know it. I've always hoped I'd get a look at it one of these days. There was an article in the local paper years ago about past tragedies in the area. The Belles were one of the families featured, but I don't remember all the details."

"I saw the whole thing," Addison said. "I saw what happened to her."

"What do you mean?"

"Sara took me back to the day it happened. There was an accident. A car ran through the stop sign, slamming into the vehicle Sara's nanny was driving. There were three of them in the car: Sara, the nanny, and a boy I believe was the nanny's boyfriend. They all died. At least, I *think* they all died."

Luke crossed his arms and sighed. "I don't like this. You *just* had the baby. We're not even home yet."

"I get it. I do. But she's made contact now, and she's confused. I need to help her."

"No, you don't. She's waited this long. She can wait a bit more."

"There's a reason she's still here, Luke. The faster I can find out why, the faster she can move on, and we can get back to our lives."

He shook his head. "Until another spirit comes along seeking your help, you mean?"

"I know it's not what you want to hear. I don't know what else to say."

Luke reached out, taking Addison's hand in his. "It's out of your control. I get it. I just want you and the baby to be safe."

"I know you do, and we will be. We're protected."

"How can you be so sure?"

She wasn't, but she believed one new item in her arsenal would provide such protection—a book left to her by her grandmother.

CHAPTER 5

The book of enchantments had been given to Addison right before her grandmother passed away. Addison clutched it in her hands and sat on the bed, staring at the embossed image in the center of the book's cover. Three women stood around a pillar of light—a grandmother, a daughter, and a grandchild, symbols of magic from one generation to another.

Given the book's weathered age, Addison had expected to find its pages filled with spells when she'd first received it, until she'd cracked it open, poring over the words written by her ancestors. The pages read like lyrical verses of music, each offering wisdom, warning, advice, and best of all—enchantment.

When Marjorie offered it to Addison, she'd said, "With this book you have all the power you can possess, everything I have."

And yet, even after taking possession of the book, she still felt a part of her was missing.

Addison closed the book, put it to the side, grabbed her laptop off the nightstand, and went to the main page of the *Rhinebeck Bee*, a long-standing local newspaper established in the thirties. In the search bar she typed: car crash, Sara Belle, Scarlett, Theo, 70s.

The inquiry yielded several results. Most interesting was a front-page story dated August 12, 1973, which included a large, black-and-white photograph of the car taken at the scene of the crash. The article read:

A young woman and child are dead, and a third person has been critically injured following a hit-and-run traffic accident five days ago at the intersection of Dawson and Nile. The two lives claimed were a young girl, Sara Belle, 6, and her nanny, Scarlett Whittaker, 20. Still in serious condition at Duke Hospital's intensive care unit is Theodore Price, 21.

State police have reported the accident took place at 4:30 in the afternoon. Scarlett Whittaker, who was operating the car at the time, was found in the driver's seat. It is believed she died on impact. Sara Belle was thrown several feet from the car and also perished at the scene. Theodore Price suffered multiple broken bones and a severe head injury, but after two surgeries in the days following the accident, doctors believe there's a good chance he may survive.

Scarlett Whittaker was traveling north when a dark blue or black truck ran a stop sign, striking her vehicle in the side. Whittaker's car spiraled out of control, crashing into a tree, where it was demolished. The unknown driver of the other vehicle fled the scene, and as of today, he or she has not yet been identified. Police are asking anyone who may have information about the hit-and-run driver or anyone in the area at the time of the crash to please come forward.

Addison combed through stories related to the crash and discovered Theo had lived. She also found a smattering of mentions on the continued search for the unknown individual driving the truck. According to the articles, the hit-and-run driver had never been identified.

Addison leaned back on a pillow and closed her eyes, recalling the moment Theo had spotted the other car. For a split second

Addison could have sworn she'd seen the driver, but his face was blurred, like he was being viewed through a kaleidoscope.

Why had he run the stop sign in the first place?

Had he seen it?

Was it intentional?

Multiple theories flooded her mind.

Maybe the other driver had been drunk at the time. Maybe he'd fallen asleep at the wheel. Or maybe the reason for the crash was something far more sinister.

A quick Google search provided Addison with a lead. Theodore Price was now sixty-seven-years old. He was married, owned an auto parts store, and he lived in Hyde Park, a short twenty-minute drive away.

Luke entered the bedroom and narrowed his eyes. "What are you up to in here?"

"Just getting some rest while the baby's sleeping," Addison said.

He scanned the bed and thumbed toward the book. "Rest and some light reading?"

Something like that.

"Sara will contact me again," Addison said. "She's scared, Luke. I'm not sure she understands what happened to her."

"Yeah, well, I came upstairs to tell you Lia's downstairs. She stopped by to see how we're all doing."

Addison had first met Lia McReedy when Addison moved to Rhinebeck and discovered some old bones on the property surrounding the manor. Lia was the medical examiner who had been assigned to the case. They'd clashed a bit at first, but over time, the pair had become close friends.

Addison found Lia in the living room, staring at a shadow box on the wall containing a vintage white cloche hat and matching lace gloves.

Lia tipped her head toward the display. "Nice. When did you get it framed?"

"About a week ago. They were Gran's."

Lia nodded. "I remember. Those were the gloves she wore the weekend of your wedding, right?"

Addison nodded.

"Marjorie was so posh," Lia said. "I've never seen a woman so stylish in their older age. She reminded me of Sophia Loren."

"She would have loved the compliment."

"How are you, and how's the baby?"

"We're both doing well."

Lia reached into her handbag and pulled out a box dressed in pink and yellow wrapping paper. "I come bearing gifts, and I was hoping I'd get the chance to hold the little one if it's possible."

"She's asleep. If you can hang around for a bit, she should be awake soon."

Lia lowered her voice to a whisper. "I'm sorry. I should have called first."

"It's all right," Addison said. "You don't need to whisper. Your timing is perfect. I was going to call you. I'm in need of a favor."

"What kind of favor?"

"The kind where I use the book Marjorie gave me."

Lia crossed her arms and leaned forward. "Are you talking about what I think you're talking about?"

"I am. A young girl made contact with me at the hospital."

Addison filled Lia in on the details.

When she finished, Lia said, "Poor thing. Where is Sara now?"

"I don't know. I haven't seen her again. I'm going to give her a bit more time, and if she still doesn't make contact, I'll summon her."

Lia raised a brow. "You and Marjorie used to do that together. Can you do it without her?"

"I think so."

"Guess you'll never know until you try. What can I do to help?"

"Any chance the police would still have the evidence they found on the day of the accident? And if so, are you able to get your hands on it?"

Lia considered the question. "We keep everything, so I'd say we still have it. It's an old case no one's interested in anymore. Shouldn't be too hard to find someone willing to let me take a look. Anything else?"

"I'm hoping something the police collected will help me piece together what I don't already know."

"Evidence was a lot different in the seventies. There are tests we can run now that they didn't have back then. If I find something of value, I'll let you know."

Addison shot Lia a wink. "Or you go one better and bring it to me."

CHAPTER 6

Belle Manor was nestled atop a steep, winding hill behind a grove of trees, making it so secluded, it was hidden from the city below. In the years since Addison had moved to the area, she hadn't noticed the manor until the day she'd gone for a hike on a dirt trail above the city. She'd followed a bird up a steep path, watched it perch on a branch, and then spread its wings and fly away. Addison had watched it soar through the sky, and then her attention diverted to a cluster of shiny, metallic objects reflecting off the sun. They appeared to be spires on top of an enormous house.

A few days later, Addison had indulged her curiosity and stopped into a local coffee shop to ask Janice Yaraskovitch, one of the town's oldest residents and a local historian, what she knew about the mysterious manor she thought she'd seen. Janice said the manor had once been considered the most lavish home in the area. Built in the late 1800s, Belle Manor was a place the upper class gathered to watch movies in its grand theater room while mingling and sipping on cocktails. The owners, Lawrence and Cecilia Belle, had both come from well-to-do families, with Lawrence's parents owning a plantation in the South. Under a great deal of pressure to remain at the plantation and take it over when his father retired,

Lawrence sought to escape. During a visit to New York City, an opportunity presented itself when he met and fell in love with an aspiring actress named Cecilia DuPont. One week later he left his home in Louisiana and relocated to New York.

According to Janice, the Belles had hosted movie nights and dinner parties on Friday and Saturday nights for a number of years, which often included the film's actors and actresses. She'd said celebrities flocked to Belle Manor because of its isolated location. It was a place they could escape, far from the public eye.

Life at Belle Manor hummed along for years before the accident. After, the parties ceased. Rumors lingered, most suggesting Lawrence and Cecilia became reclusive homebodies, fractions of the glamorous couple they'd once been.

Little was known of them now, and Addison decided it was time to find out why.

CHAPTER 7

Addison wound the car up a steep, cobblestone road, passing an open gate before she arrived at the Victorian, gothic-style manor. The manor was nothing like it had been in its youth. It was in a state of decline and disrepair. Pieces of the exterior were faded and chipped off, exposing such an overabundance of neglect, Addison wondered if the manor had been abandoned.

She parked the car and stepped outside.

It was quiet.

Eerily quiet.

Too quiet, almost.

There was no rustling of trees, no birds chirping, no animals sounding off in the distance. Addison surveyed her surroundings, taking it all in. The diabolical sound of a man's voice kicked up like a cyclone spinning around her, whispering words inside her ears.

Get out ... leave this place ... you shouldn't be here."

She spun around, searching for someone—anyone.

No one was there.

She was alone.

She headed toward the front door, stopping when the voice started again.

"*Hear what I say. You're not wanted here … WITCH.*"

Witch?

It was a label she hadn't been called before.

"Whoever you are, I'm *not* leaving," Addison said.

The voices circled around her and she pressed on, ignoring the warnings. The front door opened, and a short, elderly gentleman with a thick, gray beard and eyes too small for his large, elongated face hustled toward her, letting the door close behind him. He wore a collared shirt beneath a black sweater and dark slacks. Based on the irked expression on his face, he wasn't happy she was there.

He stabbed a finger in her direction and said, "How did you get here?"

Not expecting such a gruff welcome, Addison wasn't sure how to respond. "I … umm … drove."

"Let's try again. I'm *asking* how you managed to get through the gate. It was closed, and it was locked."

"The gate was open."

He frowned. "Nope, impossible."

"Are you suggesting I'm lying?"

"I am. I don't know you. I have no reason to believe you're telling the truth."

"Drive down and see for yourself."

He folded his arms and huffed a sigh of irritation. "Even *if* the gate was open, as you allege, there are still signs posted there."

Addison shrugged. "What signs? I didn't see any."

He rolled his eyes. "The ones stating you're entering private property. They say 'no trespassing' in capital letters."

The gate had been open when she came through, and as for the signs, she hadn't noticed any. Was it possible she'd missed them?

"I'm not sure what to say," she said. "I saw no signs."

"Now I *know* you're lying."

"I was preoccupied. It's a beautiful drive."

"The point is, you don't have permission to be here."

"Is this how you welcome all your guests?"

He glared at her like she was joking. "*Guests* are invited. *You* were not."

"I'm here to see Lawrence and Cecilia Belle. Do they live here?"

He shook his head. "Not possible."

"Why not?"

"It just isn't. Why do you need to see them, anyway?"

"Are you Lawrence?"

He laughed. "I should say not."

"Then this isn't your place, and me being here isn't your decision to make. It's theirs."

"What I say goes around here."

"And yet, when I looked into the current owners of the manor, Lawrence and Cecilia are still listed. If you're not Lawrence, you have no right to send me away. If they don't want me here, they can tell me themselves, and I'll leave."

She brushed past him and fisted a hand, preparing to knock on the front door.

The man grabbed her arm and jerked her back. "It's time for you to go."

Addison shrugged him off. "Don't touch me!"

He poked at her shoulder with his finger, "Or what? What are *you* going to do?"

"Did you live here when Sara was alive? Did you know her?"

He stepped back, surprised, like her name hadn't been spoken in so long, it had almost become unfamiliar to him.

"Sara is ... she was ... none of your business, and you need to leave. Now."

"She was killed by a hit-and-run driver, right? And the person responsible was never found."

"If you've come here to stir up the past, you won't get anywhere."

It had been over forty years since Sara's death, but the pain the man exhibited on his face was evident. He *had* known her.

"You're Lawrence," Addison said. "You were Sara's father, weren't you?"

"I … no. I wasn't. I'm not who you think I am."

"You knew her, though. I can tell."

The front door creaked open, and a woman stepped outside. She was barefoot, dressed in a white nightgown, and had long, straight, white hair. Her face was slender and pale and looked like it hadn't seen the sun in ages.

She narrowed her kind, melancholy eyes at Addison and said, "Hello there. What's your name?"

"I'm Addison. Are you Cecilia Belle?"

The woman nodded.

The man glared at Cecilia. "Say nothing, CeeCee."

"Why not? It's been ages since we've had a visitor. Can't we invite her inside? She looks cold. It's cold out here. Are you cold, Addison?"

"She's not a visitor," the man said, "and she's *not* coming inside."

"Why have you come?" Cecilia asked.

"I wanted to ask you about—"

"Nothing," the man interjected. "She was out for a drive and stumbled on our place, and she was just leaving before you came outside."

"That's not true," Addison said.

Cecilia looked confused. "Well, which is it?"

Addison glared at the man. "Why not let her decide for herself? If she wants to talk to me, what's the problem?"

"CeeCee, go back inside the house," the man said.

"I … no. I think I'd like to stay here and talk to our new friend."

"Go back into the house," he said. "Right now."

Cecilia lowered her head and frowned like a child forced to do her parent's bidding.

"Wait," Addison said. "I really need to talk to you, Mrs. Belle."

Cecilia glanced back. "Oh, that's nice. You seem nice. I'm sorry, I can't right now. Maybe another day."

Cecilia disappeared inside the manor, and the man cracked a slight grin.

She'd done what he asked.

He'd gotten his way.

"You have ten seconds to get off this property or I'm calling the police," he said.

He pulled a cell phone out of his pocket, waved it around for effect, and began counting down.

Addison backed toward the car and opened the door, catching a glimpse of what appeared to be a second, smaller house attached to the main one. Through a window on the side, Addison thought she saw a shadow at first. Then the shadow moved. A woman with her hands pressed against the window stared down at Addison, her face forlorn and tired, eyes pleading for Addison to stay. She had long, blonde hair and was dressed in similar attire to what Cecilia had been wearing.

The man counted down to five, looked at Addison, and then followed her line of sight. "What in heaven's name are you looking at?"

"The back part of the manor."

He shrugged. "What about it?"

"Who is the woman?"

He screwed up his face, looking at Addison like she was nuts, and then stared back at the house again. "*What* woman? What are you talking about?"

Addison pointed. "She's in the window. Can't you see her?"

The man groaned. "It's not a woman. It's curtains."

"A white curtain with hair? I don't think so."

"Stop playing games. Stop stalling. It won't work. There's no one there. No one has lived in that part of the house for decades."

"Why not?"

"Doesn't matter. It's not your business."

It may not have been, but there was worry in his eyes, stories he'd refused to tell. She wished she could plug him into an outlet and play his life back on a giant screen. For now, she'd have to wait. She needed to find a different way to get inside the manor walls—a way that didn't involve him.

Addison threw her hands in the air. "All right, fine. I'll leave."

"I'll head down after you and secure the gate with a new lock, just in case you decide to try something like this again."

"If you think locking me out will keep me from learning your secrets, you're wrong."

"My *secrets*?" he said. "Why would you say such a thing? What is it you think you know?"

Addison opened the car door, looked back, and said, "There's something troublesome about Sara's death. There's more to the accident than what anyone knows. There's more to this manor, too, and whether you let me in or not, I intend to find out."

CHAPTER 8

Addison drove away from the manor with more questions than answers. What were the eerie whispers of warning when she'd arrived? Who was the woman in the window? Why did Cecilia Belle look so frail? Why did it seem she was being held captive in her own house? And who was the grumpy man she'd just encountered? Whatever secrets lingered within Belle Manor, it was clear Sara was just the beginning.

Addison located the front gate at the end of the driveway and gasped. It *was* open, just like it had been when she'd driven through minutes before, only this time a woman hovered next to it, staring at Addison like she had expected her arrival.

It was Josephine, the woman Addison had met in the supermarket. Addison pulled the car to the side of the road, put her window down, and said, "Josephine? What are you doing here?"

"Waiting for you," Josephine said. "How's Amara Jane?"

"She's perfect."

Josephine pressed her hands together like she intended to pray and said, "I knew she would be. Haven't got her with you now, do you? I was hoping I'd get the chance to see her."

Addison shook her head. "She's at home with her father."

Josephine smiled. "I see. Another time, perhaps."

"When I saw you in the supermarket, I thought you were … I mean … I can sometimes tell the difference between those who are living and those who are … well …"

"Dead? It's all right. You can say it. I'm well aware of my condition."

"Sometimes people aren't."

"Not me. I was deader than a hog in a slaughterhouse last time I checked."

"When did you pass away?" Addison asked.

"Been some time, I imagine. I've lost track of just how long. It all blends together now. Day. Night. Time. Hard to tell the difference."

"There was something I wanted to ask you if we met again," Addison said.

"All right. Shoot."

"How did you know I'd be able to communicate with you in the grocery store that day?"

Josephine shrugged. "Guess you could say your daughter told me."

"I don't understand," Addison said. "She wasn't even born yet. How could she?"

"I'm not sure. All I know is that when you passed me in the aisle, your tummy was all lit up like a firefly under a microscope. I could see your daughter inside of you, and even though it was a bit of a shock, I knew you weren't like everyone else. You were different. I didn't know how, but I could tell there was something special about you, something that made you more unique than everyone else. Who are you? Or I guess the better question is, *what* are you?"

Addison considered the question. "The easiest explanation would be to say I'm an empath. I see things. Sometimes I see the past, and sometimes I see the present. I can communicate with the dead when they're in need of me, and I have the ability to make things happen sometimes, things which are, well, magical."

"What do the dead need from you?"

"I help them detach from this world and move on," Addison said.

"You're a unique woman, Addison."

"I guess. It doesn't always feel that way."

"I died there, you know, in the grocery store. Had a heart attack on the same aisle you were in when your water broke. Since my death, I've been … well … I don't know how to describe it. I'm in a middle place, somewhere between this life and the next. I seem to be stuck here."

"Any idea why?"

"I've resisted moving on, but it's getting harder and harder for me to stay." She looked down. "Just look at me. I'm wasting away. Soon there will be nothing left of me at all."

It was true. Josephine appeared much more translucent than the last time Addison had seen her. Trapped spirits were usually in limbo because of something left unresolved at the time of their death. It seemed Josephine could move on, so why hadn't she?

"Could you go to the spirit world if you wanted?" Addison asked.

"I'm not sure. Sometimes I leave this place."

"And go where?"

"I don't know. Somewhere a lot different."

"Different, how?"

"It's radiant. Everything is bright and colorful, and there are animals everywhere. I can understand people's thoughts without them saying a word."

"What happens when you're there?"

"The same thing every time. I walk toward a door. It's white. It opens, and I see my father on the other side. He grins and says he's been waiting for me. He reaches out his hand and asks me to come to him so we can be together again."

"And do you?"

"I don't. I shake my head and step back. He seems confused. He bows his head, and as the door starts to close, he disappears. Everything around me fades away, and I find myself back here again."

"Why don't you stay there?" Addison asked. "Was something left unresolved when you died?"

"It may have been," she said. "I've never been one who needs resolution for what occurred in my own life. When it comes to those I care about, it's a different matter."

It was obvious she was hinting at something.

"What can I do for you?"

"All these years, I've been waiting. I wasn't sure why. Now I know I was waiting for you. It all makes sense. *You* are my way back to Sara."

"Sara Belle?" Addison said.

She nodded. "Sara is my granddaughter. I believe she's the reason I've struggled to move on."

"Why?"

"Because I can't forgive myself for what happened on the day she died."

CHAPTER 9

I stopped by the manor to see Sara on the day she died," Josephine said. "I gave her a stuffed teddy bear I'd bought for her, and she begged me to take her for ice cream. I said I would. Then I remembered I was meant to meet up with a friend. I offered to take Sara for ice cream another day. I'll never forget the sad look on her face when she didn't get what she wanted. She wrapped her arms around the bear and buried her face into it, pouting. I felt so bad. The nanny overheard our conversation and offered to take Sara herself. At the time, I was appreciative and relieved, but it ended up being the last time I saw her alive."

"You haven't seen her since you died?" Addison asked. "I would have thought the two of you could reconnect somehow."

She shook her head. "I hoped we could be together, and I've searched for her. I never found her. You're the only one I've seen in decades."

Josephine's afterlife seemed desolate, and yet she'd stayed, hoping one day to reunite with the granddaughter she'd lost.

"I'm sorry," Addison said. "I can only imagine what it's been like for you all these years."

"Aww, well. Maybe I deserve the isolation. Instead of making Sara a priority, I ditched her to meet up with a friend. I've had a long while to think about the decisions we make as people, and the way we prioritize things. It's a shame. I would do anything to make it up to her now. If I would have just taken her for ice cream like she'd wanted, the accident would have been prevented, and she'd still be alive today."

Addison didn't agree.

"It's not your fault. There's no way to know what would have happened. If it wasn't a car accident, it would have been something else. I'm not sure we can escape our fate."

"When I saw you in the store and you saw me, I knew we were meant to connect with each other. I knew you were meant to help me, and I was right. Here you are now, at Sara's home. Why did you visit the manor today?"

An eerie feeling diverted Addison's attention. It felt as though someone was watching from the sidelines, devouring every move she made. And the air had changed, emitting a foul stench of decay.

"What is it?" Josephine asked. "What's wrong?"

"I'm not sure. Can you feel it?"

"Feel what, dear?"

"The change in the air. It's colder, and it shouldn't be, not this cold."

Josephine narrowed her eyes. "I'm not sure. It all feels the same to me."

A gust of wind rustled through the trees, kicking a mass of fall leaves off the branches. The leaves blew through the air, slapping against each other as they fell to the ground. A nearby tree wavered back and forth. Josephine glanced at it and yelled, "Move! Get out of the way! Now!"

Addison ran toward the car and crouched down on the passenger side. Glancing back, lightning struck one of the trees, igniting the trunk from within. The tree blew apart, exploding into a mass of fragmented pieces. Unsure what to make of it, Addison remained still for a time. She waited for everything to go quiet. Then she stepped out and looked around.

"Josephine?" Addison said. "Are you still here?"

"I am," Josephine replied. "I'm right behind you."

Addison turned.

"I've never seen anything like that before," Josephine said. "What do you make of it?"

"It was a warning. My second one of the day."

Josephine looked confused. "The second? When was the first?"

"I thought I heard something, voices, when I arrived at the manor. Then right before the tree caught fire, you asked me why I came here today. You're not the only spirit who's visited me. I've seen Sara."

Josephine's eyes widened. "When did you see her? Where?"

"She visited me in the hospital. I took her hand, and we went back in time, to the day of the car crash. She wanted me to see it. I'm just not sure about all the details yet, or what it all means. She wants to tell me something, but she's afraid."

"What happened after she visited you?"

"Nothing. I haven't seen her since."

Josephine shook her head. "I can't believe you relived that fateful day. The accident was shocking and cruel, a gut-wrenching scene for those who witnessed the aftermath of it all. I always thought seeing one of my children die before I did would be a burden too heavy to bear, but my grandchild? What happened to Sara was far worse than anything I could have imagined. Her death brought on an onslaught of events like stacked dominos. One day everything was in line: the next it all came crashing down. I didn't just lose a granddaughter that day. I lost my own daughter as well, mentally at least. She was never the same again."

"I saw Cecilia at the manor today."

"Oh? How is she?"

"She seemed off, detached from actual life. She tried to invite me in and was shot down by a man whose only goal was to send me away as soon as I arrived."

"What man?"

"I don't know," Addison said. "He wouldn't give me his name."

"What did he look like?"

"He was older, late seventies, I'd guess. He had a beard and a fair bit of weight on him. Not too much, but he wasn't thin."

She shook her head. "Hmm. Could be Lawrence, I suppose. When I was around him, he was as fit as a man could be. That was many years ago, though. Time may not have been kind to him."

Addison wished Josephine could have given her insight into the man's identity, but apparently Josephine had passed away long ago. The man could be anyone from Josephine's time or after her death. Addison couldn't provide more information—like a unique characteristic that Josephine might remember—because other than a snotty behavior, the man really had none. "What happened after Sara died? How did things change?"

"My daughter's zest for life diminished each day until it no longer existed. She became a recluse. If you had known her before the accident, you wouldn't have recognized the woman she became after Sara's death. There was a time when she was the biggest socialite in the city. Sara's death changed her, as it would any mother. Sucked the life right out of her. She lost her identity, relying on her husband for everything. She locked herself inside the manor, shutting herself away from family and friends."

All these years later, not much had changed, and yet Cecilia had hung on.

Josephine studied Addison's face, reading her thoughts.

"My daughter attempted suicide at least three times after Sara died," Josephine said. "The first month after Sara's death I visited her every day, trying to lift her spirits, get her out of bed and interested in life again. I thought it helped, until the day I showed up and was turned away."

"By whom? Her husband?"

Josephine nodded.

"Why didn't he let you see her?" Addison asked.

"He placed all the blame on my daughter. He said she couldn't handle my optimism. She didn't like me pushing her to be someone she had no interest in being anymore. He apologized and said it wasn't personal. She had refused to see everyone."

"Did you believe him?"

She shook her head. "Not a single word. I told him he needed to let me in. I wanted to hear it from her own lips."

"And did he allow you inside?"

"Not that day, no. He showed me to the door and suggested I give her time to heal on her own. He was sure she'd come around, and when she did, he promised to call me. I stayed away for a few weeks, stewing over it. I called a few times, and my calls went unanswered. Then I decided I needed to do something."

"What did you do?" Addison asked.

"I went to the police. I thought they would help me. It was a mistake. They said there was nothing they could do, which was a polite way of saying there was nothing they *would* do. Lawrence Belle was the most influential man in the city. No one went against him, and no one questioned him. Not back then."

Addison thought of Amara Jane. So young. So fragile. So innocent. She couldn't imagine not being part of her life.

"What did you do when the police refused to help you?" Addison asked.

"Two months came and went. I still hadn't heard from her, and I'd had enough. One night I dressed in black from head to toe and drove to this gate we're standing in front of now. I parked my car and walked the rest of the way. My plan was to slip inside and get my daughter. I made it to the front door before Lawrence caught me. I thought he'd send me away again. To my surprise, he invited me in."

It was an interesting turn of events.

"Then what happened?"

"Lawrence woke Cecilia and sent me in to see her. She asked for a glass of water. He brought it to her and then said he'd leave us alone for a few minutes to chat."

"How was she?" Addison asked.

"The best word I can think of to describe her behavior is bizarre. She wasn't herself. At first, I assumed she was still in a dark place. Now, I'm not so sure. She'd changed so much in a short period of time. I questioned her about it, and she shrugged it off. She said she was tired because she never slept. Even if it had been true, a lack of sleep wasn't the only thing that bothered me."

"What else did you notice?"

"She was pale, as white as the sheets on her bed, and she seemed confused about who I was when I first entered the room. I didn't understand it. I did most of the talking, and she offered a slight nod here and there. At times, she'd string together a garbled sentence, and I noticed her speech was slurred. It was hard to understand what she was saying."

"What did you do?"

"The only thing I could do. I told her I loved her. I said I was there for her. I suggested she might feel better if she left the manor for a time and came to live with me. Before I left, I asked her to consider my proposal. She said she would. I knew Lawrence would never go for it, not even for a short time. The next day, I made an appointment with a lawyer to see if I could petition the court to have her released into my care."

It was a risky move, and Addison admired Josephine's grit and desire to do what needed to be done to protect her daughter.

"Did her husband know of your intentions?" Addison asked.

She shook her head. "I don't believe so, not unless he was eavesdropping. I never said a word to him."

"What did the lawyer say?"

"Right before we were scheduled to meet, I stopped off at the grocery store. Ten minutes later, I died."

"How old were you when it happened?"

"Fifty-eight."

"Any prior health problems?"

She shook her head. "Not a single one."

It could have been a coincidence. She could have had a sudden heart attack, which led to her death, or Addison had just figured out something Josephine hadn't yet.

"What happened after you spoke to your daughter that night?" Addison asked. "Did you see Lawrence again before you left?"

She nodded. "He made me a cup of tea. We sat down together in the parlor, and he told me it was hard to see Cecilia suffer like she had. He apologized for not letting me visit sooner and said he had honored her wishes to be alone. He walked me to the door, thanked me for stopping by, and invited me to return the next day."

It seemed nice, too nice, all other things considered.

Addison didn't buy it.

"I have a theory about what happened to you, what *really* happened, and why you're still here, trapped between this life and the next. I don't believe Sara is the only reason."

Josephine tipped her head to the side. "I'm not sure what you mean. I've just told you what happened."

"You told me what you know. I believe there are things you don't know."

"Such as?"

"It's possible the tea Lawrence gave you was a slow release poison that didn't take effect until the next morning."

She reeled back in shock. "You think so?"

"I do. You're bouncing back and forth between this life and the next. Like Sara, your death may be unresolved. They may even be connected."

Josephine took a moment to let it sink in. "Let's say you're right. What happens now?"

"Now I find the truth."

CHAPTER 10

Addison returned home to find a ratty brown box sitting on top of the dining room table. It contained items relating to the car crash. Lia had dropped it by earlier, texting Addison to say she'd been given permission to look through it since the case was so old, and it hadn't been touched in decades. Addison grabbed the box's lid, but before she lifted it, Amara Jane stirred in the next room. Addison released the lid and backed away. The box could wait. Caring for her daughter could not.

Addison took Amara Jane into her arms, gave her a gentle kiss, and sat back on the chair, rocking her sweet child back to sleep again. She thought of Sara and how young she'd been when she'd lost her life—far too young to be ripped away from her mother.

Once Amara Jane was sleeping again, Addison placed her into the bassinet and then slid into bed beside it. Luke rolled over, produced a sleepy smile, and rubbed Addison's arm. He mumbled a question about the time. Addison said it was past midnight, and he nodded, turning to his side to doze off again. She snuggled in next to him and closed her eyes. It had been a long, tiresome day. Sleep should have been effortless.

It wasn't.

A faint glow radiated from the crack beneath the bedroom door, pulsing off and on like a siren.

How strange.

Addison's evening ritual included walking through each room of the house, making sure the doors were locked and the lights were switched off before she retired to bed. Tonight had been no different. So where was the light coming from? She tiptoed out of the bedroom, careful not to rouse her two sleeping beauties, and stepped into the hallway. Glancing around, she located the source of the light. It came from the main level of the house. She descended the stairs, pausing when she reached the bottom.

If all the lights *had been* out, it was possible they had an intruder.

For a moment, she considered backing up the stairs and waking Luke. She didn't.

She crouched down and surveyed the main floor of the house. The living room was dark. The hallway was dark. The kitchen was not. She crept to the corner dividing the living room and the kitchen and backed against the wall.

"Hello?" she whispered. "Is someone there?"

She was met with silence.

"If someone *is* there, you are trespassing, and I am armed. Step out so I can see you."

By *armed*, she was referring to the only viable weapon she'd seen before she headed out of the bedroom—a fork resting on a plate on Luke's bedside table.

"Is anyone there?" Addison asked. "Last chance to show yourself."

The house remained quiet.

Addison took a deep breath and poked part of her head around the corner. The source of the light was in plain sight, sitting where she'd left it on the table. It was the box, and it appeared to be illuminated from the inside.

CHAPTER 11

Earlier, when Addison touched the box, she'd felt a slight rush of energy. It seemed the box had awakened. When she placed her hands on the lid, she'd breathed new life into a pile of old relics which had sat on a shelf in a room, growing old beneath a blanket of dust.

Addison lifted the lid and peered inside the box. Sitting at the top was an item she recognized—the teddy bear Josephine had given to Sara. She grabbed the bear and inspected it, the stains she'd noticed before becoming obvious now. The stains were dried blood.

Addison set the bear to the side and kept digging. Next she pulled out a purse belonging to Scarlett. Inside was a pack of cigarettes, a hairbrush, several sticks of gum, and a pair of Led Zeppelin tickets. The box also contained a shirt and skirt and a small, rolled-up blanket. Beneath the blanket, sitting at the bottom of the box, was a gold, heart-shaped locket.

The locket was glowing.

Addison reached for the locket and opened it, hoping the inside would reveal something—a lock of hair, or even better, a portrait. To her dismay, she found nothing but a tiny black-and-white fragment, a remainder of a photo perhaps that had once been pressed into one of the locket's halves. Addison slipped the thin, delicate chain onto her hand, closed her fingers over the locket in her palm, and chanted a passage she'd read in the book of enchantments:

Secrets locked up nice and tight.

Show me the memories you contain tonight.

Addison blinked and found herself in a forest. She looked up, eyeing the brightness of the full moon. Unsure which way to go, or if she should head in any direction at all, she waited for the forest to come alive, hoping it would reveal its connection to the locket.

A twig snapped beneath Addison's feet. It made a sharp, popping noise. Addison jumped then sucked in a lungful of air and breathed, calming herself.

You're fine.

This isn't real.

It's a memory.

It's just a ...

In the distance the sound of footsteps approached, light and fast, followed by a woman's desperate pleads.

"Stop it!" the woman cried. "Leave me alone! Go away!"

The woman's voice was staggered and anxious. Addison searched the forest, trying to locate her. Seeing nothing, Addison raced toward the sound of the woman's voice. She ran into a clearing, and the woman appeared before her, brushing through Addison's shoulder as she ran past and crouched behind a tall oak tree.

Addison looked the woman over. She was young, early twenties, she guessed. She was barefoot, her left leg bleeding from a nasty gash just below her knee. Her long, blond hair fell in loose curls around her shoulders, and the gown she wore was familiar. Addison had seen it before on the woman staring down at her from a window at Belle Manor.

An ominous feeling of danger flooded Addison's mind.

Addison shouted, "Hey! I don't know why you're running, but you must keep going. You can't stay there. You're not safe."

But her words were of no use here.

She was in the past.

The forewarning offered would not change what was to come.

A man pushed through the clearing and looked around. He was tall and muscular and had large, broad shoulders. He wore a blue satin shirt, hip-hugging bell-bottoms, and scuffed, white dress shoes. He appeared bold and confident, and he had the slightest hint of a smile on his face—a smile that seemed to say he enjoyed the hunt, the round of hide-and-seek they were having. He clicked a flashlight on and waved it in front of him, scanning for movement between the trees.

"You've stopped running, which means you must be around here somewhere," he said. "Where are you, Libby?"

When his words were met with silence, he kept moving, swatting branches out of his way as he poked his head around each one of the trees.

"Now, now," he said. "Which one would you be hiding behind? You know, it's just a matter of time before I find you. There's no escaping me out here. I'll look all night. Why don't you make it easy on both of us? Come out, and we can talk. I know you're scared, but it's not what you think. I swear. Won't you let me explain? I'm a reasonable man. You can trust me, darlin'."

The man was anything *but* trustworthy and reasonable, and he was close to Libby's hiding spot. Too close. Three more trees and he'd find her.

Desperate for an alternate option, Libby poked her head out to gauge the distance between where she was and where else she could go. Her eyes darted around, searching for a place, *any* place. There wasn't one. She was trapped. Still, she grasped the urgency to do something, to try at least, and when the man turned his head, she darted out from behind the tree and sprinted in the opposite direction.

The man laughed. "Aww, there you are. I knew you couldn't have gone far. Not in these woods, and not without shoes."

In seconds, he was close enough for her to feel him breathing down her neck. He reached out and snatched her dressing gown. Clutching it in his hands, he yanked it back, breaking the gold locket dangling from her neck in the process. He grabbed the locket off the soil and shoved it into the pocket of his pants. Libby jerked around like a feral cat, resolute in her attempt to free herself from his grip. It aggravated the man even more. He grabbed a fistful of her hair and spun her around to face him.

Libby wasn't going anywhere.

The realization hit her, and her eyes flooded with tears.

"Aww, stop it, now," he said. "Don't turn on the waterworks. Are you trying to make me feel bad? It didn't need to be like this, you know. You were the one lurking around in the dark. If you would have left well enough alone, none of this would be happening. Guess it's fair to say you did this to yourself."

"I ... didn't ... *do* anything," she cried. "You did! You're a disgusting, awful person!"

"*I'm* an awful person? You seemed to have a different impression of me yesterday when you batted those long eyelashes at me every time you walked by. You knew what you were doing. You knew I had a wife."

"Whatever you saw, it's not what you think. And I wasn't flirting."

The man tossed his head back and laughed. "Now, if that's not the funniest thing I've heard all day. I'm not sure what you'd call it, then."

"I was only trying to be nice."

He nodded. "You *sure* were. I didn't mind. I thought it was cute."

The man leaned forward, forcing his lips against hers. "Mmm. Your lips taste like cherry pie."

"Stop it!"

"Why? It's just you and me now. We can do whatever we like out here."

"I wouldn't *like* to do anything with you."

He shrugged. "I'm not sure why you deny it. You wanted it before. I could tell."

"Let me go. Please!"

He leaned back and said, "Huh," like he hadn't thought through his next move yet.

Or had he?

"Why don't you, uhh … get on your knees, I guess." he said.

"What? Why?"

"On your knees. Now."

She refused, and he pressed his hands onto her shoulders, forcing her down.

"What are you going to do?" she asked. "Rape me?"

He tossed his head back and howled with laughter.

"It's not funny!" she said.

"Rape you? Are you crazy? I can't believe you'd suggest it. I've never forced anyone to have sex, and I'm not about to start today."

"What are you doing, then?" she asked.

"Close your eyes. I don't like the idea of you looking at me."

He pulled the flashlight out of his pocket and swung his arm all the way back. Libby glanced up just in time to see the wind-up before the pitch.

"No, please," she begged. "I won't say anything to anyone, I promise. You don't need to do this. Your secret's safe with me."

When he didn't respond, Libby stared up at him and screamed.

He bent down, staring into her face as he said, "Scream all you want, honey. It won't make any difference now."

CHAPTER 12

Addison sat at the kitchen table, holding Amara Jane in her arms. Caught up in the thoughts swirling around her brain, she replayed the previous night's events inside her head.

Luke entered the room, looked at Addison, and then at the locket sitting on the table.

He raised a brow. "Where'd you get that?"

"It was in the box Lia brought over yesterday," Addison said.

"You're looking at it like it's a hot potato."

"In a way, it is, but I've touched it already."

"And did something happen?"

"It took me for an unexpected ride."

Luke pulled out a chair and sat down, and Addison detailed the experience she'd had with Libby. When she finished, he picked up the locket and held it out in front of him.

"Well, it doesn't seem to be glowing now," he said. "Not unless you see something I don't."

Addison shook her head. "It already showed me what I was meant to see. I think it had a picture or two inside of it at one time, but there's nothing in it now. I've been sitting here thinking about how it went from being around Libby's neck, to the mysterious man's pocket, and then inside the car on the day of the crash."

"What are you going to do?" Luke asked.

Addison shrugged. "Try to figure out the identity of the man and woman I saw last night, I guess. When I first met Sara, I thought I'd help her move on and that was it, but nothing is easy when it comes to spirits, is it? Sara isn't the only one relying on me to uncover the truth. There are others caught up in all of this too."

"Speaking of *others* … what if there are others out there with similar abilities to yours? If there were, you could work together."

She had questioned the possibility many times.

"I asked my grandmother once, and she told me she'd never come across anyone else who was gifted like we are. I feel like there has to be more of us, but even if there are, I'm not sure how to find them."

CHAPTER 13

Addison spent the day with Luke and Amara Jane. She woke the next morning, thinking about the strange dream she'd had of a man she'd met several years before, a man she knew little about, who had once helped her find information on a missing woman. In the dream, he'd called out to her. She didn't know why. She only knew she needed to see him.

A few hours later, Addison parked the car outside the library in New York City. She placed Amara Jane into her stroller and wheeled her into the library. She scanned the main level of the first floor and smiled when she found the man she'd come to see. He glanced at her from behind a long, oval desk, stood, and walked in her direction, bending down when he reached her. He poked his head under the blanket covering Amara Jane and said, "Well, isn't she precious?"

"Thank you," Addison said. "It's been a while."

He nodded. "It has. I remember you."

"I was hoping you would."

He tapped a finger against the side of his head, thinking. "Let's see now. I'd guess it's been about six years or so since you were here last, but you don't look like you've aged a day."

"Your name is Larry, right?"

He frowned. "It's Barry. Close enough."

When Addison first met Barry, he'd been a fair bit larger than the man standing before her now. He'd slimmed down, but he didn't look healthy. He looked frail and unwell.

"You've lost weight," Addison said.

He patted his belly and nodded. "Yep. I had a heart attack a few years ago, and I made a lot of changes to my diet. I still eat a lot of the same food. I just don't eat as much."

"I see you're still wearing suspenders."

He looked down at the blue-and-white striped suspenders clipped to his jeans. "Yeah, it's a comfort thing, I guess. What brings you in today?"

"I need information on a missing woman."

"Last time you were here for something similar, if I recall, but you scampered out of here before I ever knew if you'd found what you needed."

"I did."

"What do you do for a living, anyway?" he asked.

Addison bent her head toward her daughter. "I raise this little one."

He laughed. "There isn't a better job in the world. You got a name?"

"She's Amara Jane."

"Amara Jane. She's a beauty, but I'm after the name of the person you want information on."

"Oh, right. I have a first name, but not a last. It's Libby."

"What time period?"

"Earlier seventies, I believe."

"Alive or dead?"

"Dead."

He stroked his chin. "Mmph. I wonder ... you happen to know what she looked like?"

"Thin and petite. Long, blond hair. She was young. Early twenties."

He glanced at his watch. "I'm off in twenty-five minutes. You think you could wait until then?"

Last time Addison visited the library, Barry had escorted her downstairs where the old newspapers were kept and then left the room, allowing her to peruse the boxes at her leisure. This time, he seemed keen to join her treasure hunt. She wondered why.

"If you'd just point me in the direction of the right box like you did last time, I should be able to locate what I need myself."

He crossed his arms. "You'd find a few things, I would guess. Depends on what you're after. If you can hang around until I'm off the clock, we can grab a cup of coffee in the café, and I'll tell you everything I know."

"Everything I need to know about ..."

"The woman you're looking for. Libby Carrington."

CHAPTER 14

Addison sipped on a cup of coffee and glanced at Barry. His phone rang. He looked at the name of the caller, excused himself from the table, and walked into the hallway, returning a few minutes later.

"You know something?" he said. "I've worked at the library for over thirty-five years now. Guess you could say it's where I've spent most of my life."

Amara Jane fussed in her stroller. Addison reached for a bottle and lifted her out.

"It's a long time to work at one place," Addison said. "You must like what you do."

"It's been good. It isn't always what I was interested in, though. When I was young, I had other ambitions. I wanted to be a cop. After I graduated high school, I entered the academy and became one."

"Here? In New York?"

He nodded.

"For how long?" Addison asked.

"A couple of years."

"Why did you switch jobs?"

Barry leaned forward, resting his arms on the table. "It wasn't for me. The first time I saw a dead body ... I, well ... threw up on the side of the road. Everyone said it was normal, and maybe it was, but I'll never get the image of the dead woman's face out of my mind. It haunts me even now. She couldn't have been more than eighteen or nineteen years old, and she had a face as pure and innocent as any I'd ever seen. I kept asking myself why anyone would do something like that to such a sweet woman."

"How did she die?"

"She was stabbed four times and left for dead."

"Did you ever find out why?"

He nodded. "Detectives caught the creep, and his excuse was pathetic. Turned out the guy was after her backpack. He assumed because she was dressed nice and had nice jewelry on, he'd find a lot of money in her bag. He was wrong. All she had was a couple of tens and a five. She had defensive wounds, which means she put up a fight, and she lost her life over it, over a measly twenty-five bucks."

"At least her murder was solved."

"Guess so, but for me, the damage had been done. Every night for the next three weeks, I dreamed about her death. I saw the guy standing there, hovering over her as if I'd been there when it happened. I'd wake up in the middle of the night in a cold sweat, and I couldn't go back to sleep again. After a couple of weeks, I swear I looked like I'd aged ten years. I drank to escape, to wash away the reality of the harsh world we live in sometimes. I realized I wasn't cut out to be a cop, and I quit."

Addison had a better stomach for it than he did, she guessed. She wasn't sure why. Her because her interactions with the dead were different. She picked up where the cops left off, solving the cases they couldn't, exacting justice for victims when they entered the afterlife. Barry seemed to be building to something by sharing his story, but she couldn't figure out what yet.

"I can't stay much longer," Addison said. "I need to get home."

"Sure, I won't keep you. I'd like to show you something."

"All right."

He reached into his pocket, pressed the screen on his cell phone, and flipped it around so she could see it.

"Is this her?" he asked. "Is this Libby, the woman you're interested in?"

Addison narrowed her eyes, taking in the woman's features. In her vision the night before, it had been hard to get a clear view of Libby's face. But her hair was unmistakable.

"Yes," Addison said. "I believe so. Where did you get this picture?"

"Off a buddy of mine. When I was a rookie, he was my FTO."

"FTO?"

"Field Training Officer. He had a lot more staying power than I did. Not long after I left, he got bumped up to detective."

"What's his name?" Addison asked.

"Harry Briggs."

"Were you still a police officer when Libby died?"

He shook his head. "I'd left the force by then, but I've kept in contact with Briggs over the years. He worked the Carrington girl's case. He never solved it, but he sure tried hard. When you came in today looking for information on her, I messaged him and asked if he could send me the photo from her file."

"What can you tell me about her?" Addison asked.

"Not as much as my buddy can."

"Anything would help."

"All right, let's think here. She went missing somewhere around 1972. The day before she disappeared, she had breakfast with her mother and then she drove to the college and attended all of her classes. After school, she went to work."

"Where did she work?" Addison asked.

"She worked for Lawrence and Cecilia Belle."

"Doing what?" Addison asked.

"She was their nanny. The Belles threw a lot of parties on the weekends back then."

"Yes, I've heard. Lavish ones."

He nodded. "Sometimes they hired Libby to stay the weekend with Sara, their daughter."

"Why did they need her for an entire weekend?"

He shrugged. "Based on rumors I heard back then, guests of the Belles frequently stayed overnight, and sometimes all weekend. The Belles had the rooms for it, and they doted on their guests, which made it easy for them to stick around. I imagine hiring someone to look after Sara allowed the Belles to be carefree so they didn't have to worry about tending to their daughter. If she needed anything, the sitter was there to take care of it."

"So the night before Libby Carrington went missing, she stayed the night at Belle Manor and looked after Sara. Then what?"

"The next day, Libby took Sara to the park. When they returned, they went for a swim in the pool and, then had dinner and headed to bed. The next morning when Cecilia went to wake her daughter, Libby was gone. She checked Libby's room, and the bed looked like it hadn't been slept in."

"Who was the last person to see Libby alive?"

"Hard to say. Sara, I imagine."

"Strange," Addison said. "You'd think at least one person would have had an interaction with her."

"Her job was to take care of their daughter, which means she may not have mingled with any of the other guests. If I remember right, Sara's room was on the first floor of the house. Guests mingled on the third, and those who stayed over slept on the second. Libby would have been on the first floor in the adjoining room to Sara's."

"What about her car? Was it gone, too?"

Barry wagged a finger in front of him. "Patience. I'll get to it in a minute. When the Carrington girl didn't return home the next morning, her mother called Cecilia Belle, and that's when the search began. Libby's mother called the police. They went up to the manor and questioned Sara's parents. Lawrence remembered seeing Libby and Sara in the pool, and Cecilia said Libby was reading Sara a bedtime story when she went in to kiss her daughter goodnight."

"What time was this?"

"You'd need to ask Briggs. I believe it was right before the party started."

"Did the police question Sara?"

Barry shrugged. "From what I heard, they tried. Her parents put a stop to it. They were afraid she'd be traumatized over the ordeal. She was young, about six or seven, if memory serves. The Belles said they'd question Sara themselves."

"And did they?"

He nodded. "Sara said the nanny read her a bedtime story. She was thirsty, so the nanny left the room to get her a glass of water. When she returned, she told Sara there was some leftover cake in the kitchen, and if Sara went right to sleep, she would set a piece aside for her to have the next day. Sara fell asleep while Libby went to get it, and when she woke up the next morning, she went into Libby's room, and she wasn't there."

The man Addison saw in her vision mentioned Libby saw something she shouldn't have. What had she seen?

"How many guests attended the party?"

"I'm not sure. They were all questioned, and to my knowledge, none of them had anything relevant to say. It's sad, you know. In the space of a year, the Belles went through their fair share of strange, unfortunate experiences. The Carrington girl disappeared, and then their daughter died in a car accident along with the replacement nanny. What a tragic story. It's no wonder their lives changed so much afterward."

A tragic story, indeed. Addison wondered if they'd brought it on themselves.

"After Libby disappeared, were there any leads? Did anyone come forward with any solid information?"

"A few things trickled in here and there. Nothing much."

"Nothing significant?" Addison asked.

"There was *one* thing. About six months after Libby went missing, her car was recovered at the bottom of Oak Hollow Lake, and since it didn't get there on its own, it was obvious the car had been sunk on purpose. Kind of a stupid place to dump to a car, if you ask me. Divers combed the lake for Libby's body. They didn't find it."

Oak Hollow was a twenty-minute drive from Rhinebeck and a little out of the way for a person trying to dispose of a car.

"Someone was involved in her disappearance, and they tried to get rid of the evidence," Addison said.

"You're right. Plus, Libby had a lot going for her. It wouldn't have made much sense for her to drop off the radar without telling anyone. After the car was found, Briggs was convinced foul play was involved. Guess we'll never know for sure."

Addison knew better.

Foul play was involved, and she'd find out how.

"Did they find any clues in the car?" Addison asked.

He shook his head. "Not a bit. The car was empty. It wasn't in great condition when they brought it to the surface, which didn't help."

Amara Jane drank the last of her bottle and cried out for more. Addison grabbed a pacifier out of the diaper bag and put it in her mouth.

"You may not have been on the case, but you know a lot about what happened to Libby."

Barry nodded. "I met up with Briggs for a drink or two many times back then. The Carrington case came up in every conversation. He assumed the worst, and it irked him when he couldn't prove it. We'd sit there for hours, poring over the evidence. The case still haunts him to this day. It's the only one he never solved."

"Did he work for the Village Police Department?"

Barry shook his head. "He was over in Saugerties. I have a question for you now."

"All right."

"Why are you interested in this case? It's decades old."

Addison thought about the best way to answer and came up with nothing. "It's … complicated."

"Complicated, how?"

"If I told you, it would be hard for you to believe."

He swished a hand through the air. "Oh, I doubt it. I've heard a lot of crazy stories in my lifetime. Try me."

None as crazy as mine.

Addison stood.

Barry frowned. "I answered your questions, and now I ask one of you, and you're going to run off on me?"

"It's a long story for another time. I'm not trying to be rude or ungrateful. If you can give me Briggs' contact information, I would appreciate it."

"Let me talk to him first, give him a heads up about our meeting today."

"All right."

Addison placed Amara Jane into the stroller and reached for Barry's hand. They touched, and a series of visions flashed through Addison's mind. She felt Barry's heart pumping, the blood coursing through his veins, his lungs, diseased and weak. She saw a yellow cottage with white trim on a street named Baskerville. Inside, Barry was standing in front of a mirror in the bathroom with powder-blue walls, coughing up blood into a tissue. He discarded the tissue into the wastebasket and gripped the edges of the sink in his hands, ogling himself in the mirror. His eyes were watery and sad, his face riddled with worry.

It pained her.

She didn't want to see any more.

She jerked her hand free, and Barry stepped back, confused.

"What just happened?" he asked. "What's wrong, Addison?"

"Nothing. I appreciate you taking the time to talk to me today."

"I mean, sure, I was glad to, but something has upset you."

Addison shrugged. "I'm all right. Don't worry about it. I have a lot on my mind."

"Call me crazy, but when I touched your hand just now, it felt like I'd stuck a fork into an electrical outlet."

Addison mustered a nonsensical, "How odd."

He ran a hand through his ashy hair. "It *is* odd, right? Well, never mind."

Addison felt bad.

She was cheating him, protecting herself instead of speaking the truth.

"Maybe it isn't odd," she said. "I don't know."

"There's something about you. I felt it the first time we met. Something different."

"Do you have any kids?" Addison asked.

"Sure do. A son and a granddaughter."

"Are they close by?"

"Not far. They live in Manhattan. Why?"

"Spend some time with them today. Maybe grab dinner together. Let them know how much you love them."

He raised a brow. "They *know* how I feel."

"You're a kind man, Barry. It was wonderful to see you today."

"Yeah, well, don't be a stranger. Come back for a visit again soon, okay? I work Monday to Friday, ten in the morning until five."

Addison nodded and walked away, stopping once to turn and wave, knowing his eyes were still on her as she made her way to the car.

There would be a next time for her and Barry, she could feel it.

And the next time would be their last.

CHAPTER 15

Addison poured a glass of lemonade and sat beside Luke in the living room. He looked at her and switched the television off. "Everything all right? Looks like you have a lot on your mind."

"I do," Addison said.

"Want to talk about it?"

"I don't want to worry you."

He ran a hand through her hair. "I'll worry more if you *don't* tell me. We're in this together, right?"

"All right. My abilities seem to be getting stronger. I'm not sure why."

He raised a brow. "In what way?"

"When I was young, I found a penny on the ground. I picked it up and had a vision of the man who'd dropped it. I saw his present, and I saw his future. I saw his death. I was too young to understand what I was seeing. I didn't know about the abilities I possessed at the time. It never happened again, not until today."

"What happened?"

"Do you remember Barry, the guy who works at the library in New York City, the one who helped me find information on Roxanne Rafferty?"

Luke crossed his arms and leaned back. "If you told me about him, I don't recall."

"I had other plans today. I was going to visit Theodore Price, the guy who survived the car crash. Then last night, I dreamed about Barry. When I woke up, I knew I needed to see him. I *knew* he'd have information on the woman I saw last night, and I was right."

"What happened?"

Addison told Luke about her meeting with Barry.

When she finished, he said, "Did you tell him about your vision?"

She shook her head.

"You don't know how long he has left to live, do you?" Luke asked.

"It's not long. It's hard, you know? Why is it important for me to see the end of his life when there's nothing I can do to change it?"

"What will you do? Will you tell him?"

"He doesn't know the exact day, but he knows it's soon. For now, I need to focus on something else."

"What if you had the dream because there's something you can do for him?"

Like what?

She already assisted the dead.

Was she now to help the living?

"I'm off, Luke. Way off. I have been ever since I touched Barry. I don't want to fear what will happen when I touch someone, but I'm not sure I'm ready to see everyone's future. It's draining enough to see their past."

CHAPTER 16

Addison needed to unwind, to return to center. While she'd been pregnant, Luke had turned one of the rooms in the house into a place of refuge, a place where she could communicate with those who had passed on. He'd even given it a name, "The Red Room," after the scarlet-colored paint Addison had chosen for the walls. Tonight was the first time she'd used it after she'd decided the best way to center herself was to return to the beginning, where it all started—with Sara.

Addison sat in the middle of a round, black rug, rested her hands on her knees, and closed her eyes. She visualized Sara, pulling out the details of the round curves in her face, the dimples on the sides of her cheeks, the pink tracksuit she wore the first time they met.

With a clear vision of Sara frozen in her mind, she said, "Sara Belle, I command you to appear."

A beam of light appeared in front of Addison. It was small at first, no larger than a knob on a door. It grew several feet in length and hovered there. Addison expected Sara to come through. When she didn't, Addison pushed her hand inside it.

"Sara, take my hand," Addison said. "Hear my voice and come toward me."

A force of energy surged through Addison's hand, and she drew it back, pulling Sara into the room with her.

Sara glanced around and then looked at Addison and said, "Hi. Where am I?"

"You're in my home," Addison said. "It's okay. Don't be scared. You're safe. Remember me?"

Sara stared at Addison a moment and nodded. "You were at the hospital. You have a baby. Where's your baby? Can I see her?"

"She's sleeping."

"Why?"

"Because it's nighttime."

Sara turned her head and gazed out the window. "I don't like night. I don't like it when it's dark."

"Do you remember what happened the last time you saw me?"

Sara nodded. "You came with me. We were in the car. Nanny was taking me to get ice cream. I was going to get chocolate chip. We didn't get ice cream, though."

"Why didn't you?"

"I'm tired," Sara said. "I want to sit down."

Sara sat on the floor, crossed her legs, and squeezed the teddy bear with her arms.

Addison sat beside her.

"Do you know why you didn't get any ice cream?" Addison asked.

"Don't make me say it. I don't want to say it."

"Don't make you say *what*, Sara?"

"I don't want to … you can't make me."

"I'm not trying to make you do anything, honey," Addison said.

"Yes, you are. Everyone tries to make me do things I don't want to do."

"I won't *ever* make you do anything you don't want to do. Okay?"

Sara stared at Addison. "You promise?"

"I promise."

Sara set the bear down next to her and said, "I'm sad. When I see the other kids in the hospital, I try to talk to them, but they never talk back. No one wants to be my friend."

"I think they would be your friend if they could see you."

"Only you see me. You and the angel."

The angel?

Was it possible someone had been watching out for her all this time?

"Who is the angel? What does she look like?"

"She wears a white dress, and she's really shiny. Even her hair is shiny. She smiles at me when she sees me, and that's how I know she's nice."

"Tell me about the angel."

"She's not a kid like I am. She's old."

To a child the age of Sara, her perception of *old* was relative.

"Where do you see the woman—at the hospital?"

Sara shook her head. "She's in the window behind my house."

It was a revelation Addison hadn't expected.

"You leave the hospital and go home to the manor?"

"Sometimes, when I think about home real hard, I close my eyes and say I want to go home. When I open my eyes, I'm there. I want to see Mommy and Daddy, but I don't."

"Why not?"

"The angel says I can't. She says I have to stay outside."

"She talks to you?"

"Well … kinda. Not with words. She says things with her mind. I know what she's thinking."

"Why doesn't she want you to go into the house?" Addison asked.

"I don't know. She doesn't tell me."

"Do you see anyone else when you're there?"

"Once there was a man in the window."

"Does he talk to you too?"

She nodded. "He asks me to open the door and let him out. I almost did one time, and then I saw the angel, and she said I shouldn't."

"Do you know the man?"

Sara thought about it. "I think so. I can't remember."

"What can't you remember?"

"I forgot what people look like."

Addison assumed the angel Sara referred to had to be Libby Carrington.

But who was the man?

Why was he trying to get out?

What would happen if he did?

"I have something to show you," Addison said.

"Oh … kay."

Addison dangled the locket in front of Sara. "Have you seen this before?"

"Umm … I don't know."

"Did someone give this to you or your nanny?"

Sara eyed the locket and then stuffed a hand inside her pocket. When she pulled it out, it was empty. "Why do you have Mr. Pickles' locket?"

"Is Mr. Pickles the name of your bear?"

"Uh-huh."

"Who gave the locket to you?"

Sara turned her shoulders in. "I don't know."

"You were looking for your nanny when I met you. I want to help you find her. Would you like to be with her again?"

Sara's eyes lit up, and she nodded. "Yes, please. She's nice."

"I'm not sure where to look for her. Can you help me?"

"I think she's at the hospital."

"Why would she be there?"

"I saw her after the bad thing happened."

"The bad thing … do you mean the car crash?"

"Uh-huh."

"What did Scarlett say when she came to see you?"

"She laid next to me in my bed and said not to worry. She said she had to leave, but she would come back to get me. She never came back. She left me there all alone. I waited a long time, and then you came."

"You waited in my hospital room?"

Sara nodded. "It looks different now. It has pretty colors on the wall. When I was there, I floated over the bed, and I could see myself."

Sara had wtinessed the moment her spirit detached from her body, the separation between her physical self and her soul.

"What did you see when you were floating?" Addison asked.

"I saw my nanny. She gave me a hug. She was crying."

"Why was she crying?"

"Because she had to leave. A nice lady came to get her. My nanny said she couldn't go yet. She couldn't leave without me. The lady said she had to go because it was time. My nanny said she was sorry she couldn't stay longer. She told me she'd come back, and then she walked through the door, and it turned into a wall again."

"Do you remember Libby, the nanny you had before Scarlett?"

Sara thought about it. "Yeah. Kinda."

"Can you tell me about the last night she slept over at your house, the night she went missing?"

Sara was no longer listening. She tensed, and her eyes shifted to the corner of the room.

"What is it?" Addison asked. "What's wrong?"

Sara struggled to speak, and then said, "Do you hear it?"

Addison looked over.

No one was there.

They were alone.

"You're safe here," Addison said. "Everything is going to be all right."

Sara wasn't convinced. "I have to hide."

"Why? What are you worried about?"

"I … I'm … I don't want to be here anymore."

"Why not?"

"He doesn't want me here, talking to you. He said I need to stop."

"Who says you need to stop?"

"I don't know. I can't see him. I only hear what he says in my mind."

Sara's spirit began to fade, the light ebbing from inside her.

"Wait!" Addison said. "Please. Don't go. Let me help you."

Her words came a moment too late.

Sara was already gone.

CHAPTER 17

Addison opened the book of enchantments and flipped through the pages until she found one containing several lines of verse and a poorly drawn sketch of an owl. The owl was Addison's spirit animal, an alter she transformed into when the need presented itself. She set the book on her lap, focused on the words written on the page, and chanted:

Ancient mothers far and near
Heed my voice, lend an ear
Give me wings, and allow me flight
Protection and the gift of sight
As you guide me toward the present

Addison closed her eyes, thought of Belle Manor, and released the book. It slipped through her fingers onto the floor. When her eyes opened, she felt the night's brisk, cool breeze, and she found herself in midair, hovering over the manor. Through the moon's cascading light, she caught a faint glimpse of herself in the manor's window.

She'd done it.

She'd transformed into an owl.

Addison flapped her wings, angling herself toward the window ledge. The window was open, not by much, just enough for her to duck beneath it. She stuck the landing and bobbed her head beneath the glass, trying to nudge the window open a bit more. Three quarters of the way through, her backside became stuck on the window latch.

Don't freak out.

Everything will be all right.

But everything *wasn't* all right.

Addison rocked her body back and forth, squeezing beneath the crack in the window until she broke free, the force so strong it launched her inside. She tumbled onto the floor, shaken, but unharmed.

Voices echoed from the manor's lower level.

"Did you hear that?" a man asked.

"Yeah," a woman said. "It sounded like it came from upstairs."

"I'm sure it's no big deal," the man said. "I bet it's just a—"

"You don't know what it is or isn't until you check it out," the woman said. "We can't just assume everything is fine up there. She could be hurt. Go check on her."

The man sighed. "All right, fine. I'll go."

"Wait," the woman said. "If it's not her, and it's something else, you should take this."

This?

What was *this?*

A bat?

A gun?

A knife?

Worse?

Addison wasn't waiting around to find out.

She scampered out the door toward a dim light coming from inside a room on the opposite end of the hall. She entered, looked around, and froze, shocked to find Cecilia Belle laying on a bed, dressed in the same nightgown she'd worn the last time Addison saw her.

Cecilia pushed a pair of glasses over the rim of her nose and blinked down at Addison. It was too late. She'd been seen. Addison's gaze shifted left to right, looking for an alternate means of escape. There wasn't one, and the sound of the man's heavy footsteps ascending the stairs meant he was close.

There was no place left for Addison to go.

Without uttering a word, Cecilia grabbed a mug off of her nightstand, tipped the liquid out, leaned down, and placed the mug on its side on the floor, a gesture Addison found peculiar.

All these years living like a muzzled dog has rendered her insane.

Cecilia waved Addison closer. "It's all right, my feathered friend. I won't hurt you. Come here. Get behind the bed. Hurry now. You must do what I tell you. There isn't much time."

Cecilia had spoken to Addison as if she expected her to understand what she'd just said.

Do what she says, or don't?

I have no other options, no means of escape.

With a great deal of reluctance, Addison did as she was told.

A man entered the room seconds later.

"Yes?" Cecilia asked. "Come to clean up my mess, have you?"

"I … what happened in here?" he stammered.

"Who knows? My arms must have been flailing about while I slept, and I knocked the cup onto the floor. Doesn't matter. It's just water, anyway. I'll clean it up."

The man sighed. "I'm here now. I'll do it."

"Like I said, there's no need. It's nice to take care of things myself once in a while."

Cecilia opened the drawer on her nightstand, removed a handkerchief, and bent down, blotting it over the water. She looked back at the man and said, "Why are you carrying an umbrella? It's not raining."

"I … I was just … it doesn't matter," the man said. "I heard a noise and came to check it out."

He turned and left the room.

Cecilia stayed silent for a minute, and then said, "Stay there, my friend. I've known him a long time, and I don't think he's done with me just yet."

Addison held her position. Cecilia may not have been lucid, but she was right. Minutes later, footsteps swished along the floor toward them, and the man revisited the room.

"A mop?" Cecilia said. "You're being a bit ridiculous don't you think? A splash of water won't do much damage."

"It will preserve the floor," he said.

"The *floor* is fine. At any rate, hand me the mop. I'll do it."

The man breathed a sigh of frustration. "What's gotten into you tonight?"

"Whatever do you mean?"

"You haven't been this chatty in months."

"Who knows? Maybe I'm starting to feel like myself again."

From her hiding spot, Addison saw a man's hand scoop one of the pill bottles off the nightstand. He jiggled it back and forth as if gauging how many pills remained.

"How have you been feeling the last several days?" he asked.

"Fine. Why?"

"Do you think your meds are still working?"

"How the hell should I know? You have me taking an entire drugstore full of pharmaceuticals. I'm sure they work the same way they always have."

"It's not true. You take what you need, nothing more."

"Of course, it's true. No need to lie about it."

"Doctor Farnsworth is stopping by tomorrow. I'd like him to assess you again. It's been a while since he's checked you out. Let's see what he has to say."

"See what he has to say about what?"

"Have you taken your sleeping medication tonight?"

"Not yet. I dozed off about an hour ago, though, without it."

"You need to take it. I've brought you another glass of water so you can."

The man sat on the edge of the bed. From Addison's hiding spot, she had a slight view of his face. If he angled his head a bit more to the right and glanced down, he'd see her.

"I've been thinking it may be time to up your dosage again," he said, "or even switch you to something else. It's possible you're so used to the medication you're on, since you've been taking it for a while, that it's not working like it should anymore."

"How would you know whether it does or doesn't work?" Cecilia asked. "*You're* not the one taking them. I told you. I feel fine. Best I've felt in years, in fact. I'm not interested in seeing Farnsworth tomorrow or any other day. He's pushy, and I don't like it."

There was a heap of dissatisfaction in Cecilia's tone. It was easy to understand why. The man spoke to her like she was a foolish child, incapable of deciding what was best for herself, and though Cecilia was several marbles short, she articulated her words with precision. Maybe *that's* what had the man worried. If the meds didn't have the effect they once did, and Cecilia became herself again, what would it mean for him, a man who seemed to have questionable motives?

"I understand Farnsworth isn't your favorite person," he said. "Let's not worry about him tonight. You get back to sleep now, and we can talk again in the morning after you've had some rest."

Or when she was a lot more doped up.

"I don't see what more there is to say," Cecilia said. "I'm not changing my mind."

He stood and shuffled toward the door. "I'll leave you now."

"Are you off to bed too?"

"Not for a while. I'm going to watch the news on television first. Why? Do you need anything? I can bring you a cup of tea if you like."

"A hot toddy would be nice. A wee splash of bourbon sounds perfect right about now."

"I … don't think that's a good idea."

"You don't think *anything* is a good idea anymore," Cecilia said. "You're a stuffed shirt nowadays."

"I don't want it to be this way. You're in poor health. I'm only trying to do what's best for you."

"We never sleep in the same bed anymore," Cecilia said. "I don't understand why. Why can't things go back to the way they used to, the way they were before—"

"We've been over this several times. You snore, which makes it impossible for me to get a decent night's rest."

"So you say, although I can't remember snoring a day in my life."

"You're asleep. You wouldn't know."

"Perhaps," Cecilia said.

"Goodnight, then," the man said. "I'll be up with breakfast in the morning."

"Yes, you will. Breakfast and my morning cocktail of pills. Nine o'clock on the dot. As usual."

He walked out, closing the door behind him. Cecilia jostled around in bed, and then the room went silent. Addison assumed Cecilia had forgotten about her and given in to sleep. It wasn't long before she had an answer.

"Feathered friend?" Cecilia said. "Are you still there? Come on out and let's get a good look at you."

Addison hopped onto the bed. She stared into Cecilia's eyes, vacant voids of nothing. What light she'd once had seemed to have been replaced with a sense of indifference.

"This is a real treat," Cecilia said. "I don't believe I've ever seen an owl this close before. No, I'm sure I haven't. Have you wandered far from your home in the forest? Have you lost your way? Is that how you ended up here tonight?"

Addison's eyes shifted to the plethora of pill bottles on the nightstand. In all, there were seven. Why did she need so many different prescriptions? It was no wonder Cecilia acted loopy. She couldn't possibly have needed them all.

"Lawrence is a pain sometimes, isn't he?" she said. "I try talking to him, but it always proves difficult. Most days, he's not up for conversation. Tonight is the most we've talked to one another in a long time. I think so, at least. In truth, I don't know. I think I forget from one day to the next."

Addison blinked.

Cecilia shook her head and laughed. "Sometimes I feel like I'm going mad in this old place. I mean, look at me. I'm talking to an owl, for heaven's sake. You're probably not even real. I'll bet you're nothing more than a figment of my imagination."

Without warning, Cecilia swept her hand through the air, knocking Addison off the bed. Addison flew through the air and fell to the ground, worried Lawrence would return to the room again. It was possible the television would be loud enough to spare her this time.

"Oh no," Cecilia said. "My goodness. What have I done? I'm sorr—"

Cecilia poked her head over the side of the bed and Addison glanced up. Eyes wide, what little color Cecilia had drained from her face. In a mirror on the opposite wall, Addison learned why, gasping as she caught a glimpse of her pale, freckled skin.

"Please," Addison said. "I don't want Lawrence to come up here again. I can explain."

But how?

How could she?

Cecilia's mouth dropped open, but no sound came out.

"Please," Addison said. "Don't scream. Don't call for anyone. If you could just allow me to—"

Cecilia cupped a hand over her mouth and said, "You were just covered in feathers, and now you're… I can't … I can't believe it's *you*."

CHAPTER 18

Addison was naked—stark naked—and had somehow transitioned back into her human form after the force of Cecilia's hand swatted her off the bed.

"I must be hallucinating again," Cecilia said. "None of this is real."

"I'm sorry," Addison said. "I'm sure you're confused. I don't mean to frighten you."

Cecilia wasn't listening. She was staring at her trembling hands, mumbling to herself. "I could have sworn there was an owl in my room just now, and yet, it's you, the woman who visited us earlier. You're lying on the ground in front of me like I could reach out and touch you. It's been some time since I've imagined things that aren't there … unless you *are* real, and there's some sort of explanation for all this. It's just, you were a … and now you're … and you don't have any clothes on."

Addison didn't have a clue how to fix her current predicament. She could feed into Cecilia's theory of hallucination, she supposed. While an easier option, it seemed cruel to exploit her condition.

Addison came to a sitting position and pulled her knees in front of her, crossing her arms over her breasts in an attempt to cover herself.

"I'd like to explain," Addison said. "First, do you have any clothes I can put on—something I can borrow tonight and return to you later?"

Cecilia lifted a finger in the direction of the closet. "In there."

Addison walked to the opposite end of the room, pulled the door open, and stared at a row of nightgowns. They were similar in style but varied in color. She pulled one off the hanger and slipped it over her head.

"I have imagined you," Cecilia said. "Haven't I? I'm in a strange dream. Right?"

Addison was in two minds about how to answer. The ethical side of her wanted to confess, to tell the truth, but what would happen if she did?

"Thank you for the clothes," Addison said. "Do you imagine things often?"

"I don't know. I never thought I did. Lawrence swears the things I say I've seen aren't real."

"What do you see?"

"It's not just about what I see, it's about what I hear. There are strange noises in this house at night. Voices I don't recognize. There's a woman. Her tone is shrill and squeaky like a mouse caught in a snake's fangs. It's a miracle I can hear at all because of her."

"Other than yourself, how many people live here?"

"It's only Lawrence and me."

"Do you have any visitors?"

"My friend Flora stops by every day."

"Where does she live?"

Cecilia shrugged. "Not far. I can't think of the name of the street."

"Have you told Lawrence about the woman's voice you hear?"

She crossed her arms in front of her. "I used to tell him. I don't anymore. It's a waste of time. He doesn't believe me."

"I do. I heard a woman talking to someone downstairs when I arrived. Why does Lawrence have you taking so much medication?"

Cecilia scooped a few of the bottles off the nightstand and inspected them. "It's funny. I don't even know what most of these are. He says they all do different things. One helps me sleep, another keeps me from losing my mind more than I already have, and another is supposed to help me feel better, even though nothing does. I almost died, you know."

"What happened?"

"I've tried to kill myself a few times. Once, I almost did. All I've ever wanted is to be with my daughter again. Sara was our miracle child. I was infertile. We tried to have a baby for years. I'd almost given up hope, and then the doctor gave me the best news of my life."

"Doctor Farnsworth?"

"Heavens, no."

Addison walked to the bed and sat down. "I'm sorry for all you've been through."

Cecilia raised a brow. "Why are you here, haunting my dreams? What is it you want?"

"To talk to you about Sara."

Cecilia stretched a blanket over her body and rested her head back onto a pillow.

"I heard the person who crashed into Scarlett's car was never caught," Addison said.

"You're right."

"I have the box of evidence the police gathered at the scene of the accident. Forensics has come a long way. Maybe the person responsible for Sara's death could be brought to justice now."

"Justice won't bring her back to me, so why does it matter?"

"Even after all this time, the person who caused the accident doesn't deserve to get away with it."

"I'm curious, what did you find in the box?"

"A locket," Addison said.

"What does it look like?"

"It's gold and shaped like a heart. It's smooth on one side and has a series of smaller hearts embossed on the other. Have you seen it before?"

Cecilia drummed her fingers on the bed, thinking. "Sounds similar to one our nanny wore the night she disappeared."

"Scarlett or Libby?"

"Libby. She was a simple girl. She never wore much jewelry, so it stood out. I asked her about it. She said her best friend had given it to her the day before as an early birthday present. How would it have made its way into the evidence box?"

"Good question."

"I feel for the poor girl's mother. I don't know which is the lesser of two evils—losing your daughter the way I lost Sara, or losing your daughter and she's never found. I have a certain amount of closure, at least, not that it makes much of a difference. Pain is pain. There's no getting around it. There's no escaping it, either."

"Did you see Libby the night of the party?" Addison asked.

"Of course. I spent some time with her before she put Sara to bed."

"How did she seem? What was her behavior like?"

"No different than usual."

"Did many guests attend the party the night she disappeared?"

She gave Addison a strange look. "I can't even remember what I ate for dinner tonight, let alone try to recall who came to one of our parties all those moons ago."

"There was a man at the party the night Libby disappeared. He had a muscular build and wore a blue satin shirt and flashy white shoes."

"It was a dressy period of time. Sounds like every man who visited during those days."

"Do you keep any photos from your parties?"

"I'm sure some still exist, although I'm not sure where."

Cecilia shifted her gaze to the door, eyeing it like she worried someone may have been on the opposite side. Had Lawrence returned? Was he lurking outside the door? She'd heard no footsteps in the hall, nothing to indicate he was nearby, listening. If he *had* been listening, Addison was sure he would have come inside by now.

Cecilia grabbed Addison by the wrist.

"What's wrong?" Addison asked.

"This isn't a dream, is it? You're here, now, talking to me."

"I'm here."

"Did I just wake up? I didn't see you come in. I seldom have visitors at night."

It was like someone had taken an eraser and wiped the last thirty minutes from Cecilia's mind. Addison snatched one of the pill bottles off the nightstand and studied the label. Donepezil. She'd never heard of it. She replaced it and went for another, stopping when Cecilia jerked her head toward the door again.

"What are you worried about?" Addison asked.

"The faceless man."

"Faceless? What do you mean?"

"He stands over me, looming in the darkness while I sleep. I wake in the night and there he is, staring down at me. I never see his face, not all of it. But I see his expression. It's ominous, like he wants to smother me with my own pillow."

"Is he alive or dead?"

"Dead, I think. He's something evil."

Some of Cecilia's behaviors were starting to make sense. When Addison had transformed from an owl to a human, Cecilia hadn't screamed like Addison thought she would. It seemed Addison wasn't the only unusual visitor.

"What do you think the man wants?" Addison asked.

She rolled onto her side. "I don't know. His eyes pierce the darkness. They're unforgiving and cold. I feel we know each other."

"Has he ever harmed you?"

She tugged the sleeve of her gown up a few inches, revealing a two-inch gash.

"I wake up to these now and then," she said. "They're never too bad. Still …"

"Let me guess, Lawrence thinks you do this to yourself?"

"Of course, he does. Anything else would suggest a belief in the afterlife. He's an atheist and far too practical to consider such things. He believes when we die, we're dead. End of story."

"Beyond scratches, does the man do anything else?"

"He taunts me, feeds into my fears, and at times, he destroys things." Cecilia tipped her head toward the dresser. "Top drawer. See for yourself."

Addison crossed the room and opened the drawer. Inside was a series of photos of Cecilia in a wedding dress. Every photo had been torn, severing Cecilia from everyone else. Addison placed the photos back in the drawer, returned to Cecilia's bedside, and took her hand.

"I believe what you say is happening to you," Addison said. "If your mother was still alive, she would remind you that while Lawrence is your husband, he doesn't own you."

"He may as well. I'm no good anymore, not even to myself."

"When your mother came to visit after Sara died, did you ever refuse to see her?"

Cecilia shook her head. "Of course not. Why would I?"

"Lawrence told Josephine you didn't want to see her, or anyone else."

"Why would he … no … I don't believe he would say such a thing."

"Your mother didn't agree with what was happening here."

Cecilia closed her eyes and clenched her hands. "My mother thought if she took me away from this place, away from all of the constant reminders of Sara, I would start to heal. And then my mother was taken from me too. She died, and I was angry … so angry … I …"

Exhausted, Cecilia succumbed to sleep. Addison wanted to shake her, to hear the rest of what she had been trying to say. Instead she stood and draped another blanket over Cecilia. She reached over to switch off the bedside lamp, and Cecilia's eyes flashed open.

"You must go," she said.

"Why?"

Her eyes darted around the room. "I feel him. He's almost here. Leave this place. Leave now."

Addison searched her mind, trying to recall the words of a protection spell she'd seen in the book of enchantments. She opened her mouth, but snapped it closed again when the window blew open and a dark mist flowed inside. A foul odor of rotting decay swirled around Addison, and with it, a thick, black fog coiled around Addison's body like a boa constrictor.

Fingers spread, Addison forced her hands through the mist. The haze of black dispersed throughout the room, forming again in the corner. It twisted back and forth, writhing and growing, and then molded into a silhouette of a man.

Addison walked toward him.

"Who are you?" Addison asked. "Why do you return to the manor night after night? What do you want with Cecilia?"

Laughter echoed from within the silhouette's core.

He mocked her like she was nothing, no match for him.

"You may be darkness, but I am light," Addison said.

"You lie," he growled. "I feel the darkness inside you, and you feel it too."

"Your time plaguing the manor is over. Leave, demon."

"I'll *never* leave," he hissed. "But *you* will."

He shot forward, wrapped a hand around Addison's neck, and squeezed. She swished a hand through the air in an attempt to break him apart, but he held firm, the pressure mounting.

A woman's voice rang through the wind, "Harness your power, Addison. Believe in it. Believe, and he cannot hurt you."

A shimmering orb burst through the window, plowing through the man's hand.

"Demon, be gone!" a woman said.

The hand broke apart, dispersing into air until it was gone. Addison looked around, trying to locate the source of the sound she'd heard. Whoever the mysterious woman was, she was gone.

CHAPTER 19

Addison woke the next morning with an intense feeling of sadness. It had been a short time since she'd left Barry. He still hadn't forwarded Briggs' information, and she had a good idea why.

She fed and dressed Amara Jane, gave her to Luke, and went for a drive. Two hours later, she parked in front of a yellow house with white trim. She walked to the door and knocked. A taller-than-average man in his early twenties opened the door and put his hands on his hips. "Yeah?" was all he said. He had bushy eyebrows and long brown hair, and wore a shirt displaying the cities Aerosmith had visited on their "Get a Grip" tour in 1993.

"Does Barry live here?"

"He can't come to the door right now," the man said.

"I'd like to see him."

"He's, uhh … not well."

"I know. I heard."

"I mean, he's too weak to get out of bed."

"Why isn't he at the hospital, then?"

The guy shrugged. "I've tried to get him to go. He refuses."

A young girl wrapped her arms around the man's leg and poked her head out the side, grinning at Addison.

"Hi," she said. "What's your name?"

"I'm Addison."

"That rhymes with my name. I'm Madison." She looked up at the man. "She can come in, Daddy. She's all right."

He looked at his daughter and tried to keep a straight face. It didn't last. He cracked a smile, patted her on the head, and said, "She's all right, is she?"

"Yep," the girl said. "She's nice."

"You don't even know her."

Addison pressed a hand to her lips in an attempt to stifle her own laughter. "I assume Barry is your father and this sweet girl is his granddaughter?"

"Who are *you*?" he asked. "How do you know my father?"

"We met at the library several years ago. If I could see him, even for a few minutes, it would mean a lot to me."

He ran a hand along his jawline, thinking. "I have a better idea. I'll tell him you're here, and if he wants to see you, you can come in."

He pushed on the front door like he intended to close it, but it remained open a crack. A minute later he returned and said, "I'm Tim. Come on in."

Addison walked inside.

"It's just … he's not good, you know?" Tim said. "I don't think he should have visitors, but he wants to see you."

Addison placed a hand on Tim's shoulder. "I'm sorry for all you're going through."

Tim turned away, blinking back a pool of tears. "I thought I'd be ready for it. I mean, he said he didn't have long a few months ago. Guess I hoped it wouldn't happen this fast."

"Not long ago, my grandmother died. I understand what it feels like to lose the one you love. Even though she's no longer here, I feel her, and you'll feel him too."

He shrugged. "Guess so. Anyway … umm …" He gestured down the hall. "Second door on the right. He wants to see you alone, so you go on ahead."

Addison entered Barry's room, surprised to see how frail he looked from the man she'd seen such a short time before.

Barry attempted to smile. "I'm glad you came. How did you know where I live?"

"I have my connections." She walked to the bed and sat down. "I'm sorry, Barry. I wish there was something I could do."

"Who knows? Maybe you can."

"Maybe I can, what?"

"Let's play a game, a getting-to-know-you game."

"What did you have in mind?"

"I'll tell you a secret, and you tell me one."

It seemed like an odd request.

"I … don't know."

"Oh, come on," he said. "I'll even go first."

She paused, then said, "Sure, why not?"

"When you took my hand when we last met, I saw something."

He couldn't have.

Could he?

"What did you see?"

"If I had to explain it, I guess I'd say I saw what people refer to as *the other side,* a life beyond this one. I saw myself in it. Ever since I was diagnosed, I've feared death. I think it's natural, to fear the unknown, the things we know nothing about. It's human nature. We spend our lives afraid of a lot of things. But once I saw where I'm going, my perception changed. I'm not afraid anymore. I'm at peace now. I'm ready to let go."

Addison smiled. "I'm glad."

"I never thought I'd get the chance to thank you, but here you are."

"Thank me for what?"

"For the chance to see my destiny. I believe *you* did that for me.

You made it happen. What I don't know is how you did it. Indulge a man's dying wish and tell me. Please?"

Addison walked to the bedroom door and closed it. She returned to Barry's side and said, "I often find ways to disguise who I am because if I share the truth with others, most won't understand. People have a hard time accepting things they can't comprehend. It makes people like me outcasts, weirdos who claim to be someone others assume we're not. Not everyone can handle the truth, no matter how much they think they want it."

"I can. Tell me who are you, Addison. Won't you please?"

Who was she?

Some days, she didn't even know.

"The simple explanation is I see things," she said. "I have visions. I see into the past, and on occasion, I see the future. I see those who have passed on, those stuck between this life and the next, and I help them get there."

He stared at her without changing his expression, like she had told him what household chores she'd done for the day. "How interesting. Is there a name for what you are?"

"If there is, I don't know it. I'm an empath, I guess, or a medium. The women in my family have unique abilities. We're gifted, but I've never had anyone tell me they saw the afterlife when we touched before. You're the first. Ever since my grandmother's death, I've experienced things I hadn't before, things I never thought possible. It makes me nervous at times. I'm still trying to figure it all out."

"Don't be nervous. You're blessed to have such talents."

"I suppose I am."

"Can you do something for me? Can you cross me over into the next life?"

"I can't do things like—"

"I believe you can. I know it."

If she could, she didn't know how.

"I appreciate your belief in me, but I can't do what you're asking."

He sighed. "Can't blame me for trying. I've seen what's waiting for me when I leave this tired, old body, and it's ... well, worth dying for to get there. Believe me."

She believed.

"By the way, Briggs came by this morning," he said. "We talked about your interest in the Carrington girl's case. He'd like to meet with you. You should give him a call."

"I don't have his number."

Barry attempted to lift a finger and failed.

"It's okay," Addison said.

"No, it isn't. He wrote it on a piece of paper. It's on the nightstand."

Addison located the scrap paper, picked it up, and slid it into her pocket.

"Can I get you anything before I go?" she asked.

"You can tell my son I need him."

She poked her head into the hall. Tim was close, hovering like he was waiting for permission to come back in.

Tim approached Addison and said, "Is everything okay in here?"

"Your father is asking for you," she said.

"Come over here and sit by me, son," Barry said.

Tim wiped a tear from his cheek, sat down, and took his father's hand.

"Dad," Tim said, "let me take you to the hospital."

"Don't need it," Barry said. "All I need right now is you. I love you, son. I hope you know how proud I am of you."

He seemed to know he didn't have long.

In an attempt to give Tim more time with his father, Addison headed for the door.

"Addison," Barry whispered.

She turned. "Yeah?"

"One more thing before you go," Barry said. "Take my hand, please."

She stared at his hand, and at him, knowing what he expected, what he thought would happen when she did. He'd be disappointed.

"Please, Addison," Barry said. "Take my hand and then you can go."

She nodded, crossed the room, and reached for his hand.

"Thank you," Barry said. "Thank you for being here today, for indulging an old man. It means a lot to me."

Barry's eyes drifted closed, and his head sagged to the side.

Tim shot out of his seat. He bent down, shaking his father. "Dad? Dad! Can you hear me? Dad! Say something."

"I'm sorry, Tim," Addison said. "I think he's gone."

CHAPTER 20

Addison nursed her jitters by sipping on a cup of hot chocolate. Briggs sat across from her. He had thick, gray hair, a salt-and-pepper mustache, and a pea-sized mole on his right cheek in the shape of the state of Florida. No matter how hard she tried, and how rude it was to stare, she couldn't peel her eyes away from it, and at the moment, it took her mind off everything else.

Briggs stabbed a fork into a chunk of cherry pie. It dangled partway off the fork while he said, "I hear you were with Barry when he passed. What was that like?"

There it was in his opening line, a topic Addison didn't care to discuss.

"You're not the sentimental type, are you?" she asked.

"I have a heart, and it beats just like everyone else's. I may lack the aptitude to communicate with words you would deem appropriate in these kinds of circumstances. Doesn't mean I don't care. It means I've seen my share of death in my lifetime, and I suppose you could say I've become a bit callused to it. I loved the guy, though. He was a good friend."

"It was hard to watch him take his last breath," she said. "But at least he's at peace now. Did you know?"

"Barry was on his way out? Yup. I knew. Cancer's a real bitch, isn't it? Horrible way to go."

"I liked him. He was a nice guy. It's too bad he's gone."

"From what he told me, he had a lot of respect for you."

Barry inched his glasses over the rim of his nose, swallowed the last piece of pie, and leaned back, rubbing his belly. He squinted at Addison in a way that made her feel like the interrogation had commenced.

"What's your interest in the Carrington girl?" he asked.

"I heard about the case, and I'm curious about what happened."

Briggs was clever, *too* clever, which meant her answer wasn't up to par. She gave it two out of five stars at best. And everything about him was intimidating, which also didn't help.

"That's all it is, huh … curiosity?" He leaned forward. "What makes you curious about a young lady who died before you were even born?"

She'd need more meat on the bone if she expected to get into his good graces.

"Some years ago, I inherited a house after my mother died," she said. "Not long after, I learned a young woman had died there. For decades, no one knew what happened to her until I renovated the place and … well, found her body in the process. Putting her to rest woke something in me, I guess you could say. I've had an interest in unsolved murders ever since."

"Why not become a police officer instead of nosing around on your own?"

"I prefer nosing. It suits me."

The waitress scooped Briggs' empty plate off the table and said, "All good here?"

Briggs eyed Addison. "You need anything else? Don't be shy. Get whatever you like. Lunch is on me today."

Addison raised her mug. "Another hot chocolate, please."

"You sure?" he asked. "Pie is real good today."

"I'm not sure I can stomach anything sweet right now."

Briggs handed Addison's empty mug to the waitress and said, "I'll have another piece of pie. I'm guessing we'll be here for a while."

The waitress nodded and walked away.

"So, Addison, the girl who likes to solve her own mysteries," Briggs said, "after talking to Barry, I did some digging. Since you moved to the area, you've been connected to three cold cases in six years in this state, all of which have now been solved. I'm guessing that's *not* a coincidence."

She shrugged. "Maybe I have a knack for finding the truth."

"Or maybe there's something you're not telling me."

In an attempt to take the heat off herself, she switched to the reason for her visit.

"I hoped you could tell me what you know about Libby Carrington's disappearance," she said.

He wagged a finger in the air. "Whoa, hold on now. We're still in the 'getting to know you' phase of our relationship. You wouldn't hold someone's hand before your first dance, would you?"

Briggs two points. Addison zero.

"What do you want to know?" she asked.

"Tell you what, let's start by me sharing something with you, and then you do the same in kind."

"Okay."

"Five months after the Carrington girl went missing, I knew no more about what happened to her than I did in the first five days. There was a fair amount of pressure from all sides. My worst fear was what we always fear in my line of work—that her case would go unsolved, and I'd never be able to give her family the answers they needed. I was desperate, and when you're desperate, sometimes you do things that seem a bit on the crazy side. I didn't care anymore. All I wanted was to get to the truth."

"What did you do?"

"I heard about a woman who lived in a remote area outside of the city. She was a lot more *connected* than most people, I guess you could say."

Addison pictured a wealthy member of elite society with her ear to the ground. "Connected, how? To the Belle family, or the movie industry?"

He shook his head. "Connected in more of a spiritual way. A psychic. She was said to have visions. When I first heard about her, I thought it was a load of crap. I assumed she was nothing more than a scam artist out to make money. And then a detective friend of mine said she helped him solve one of his murder cases."

"How?"

"She was able to pinpoint the location of the body, and what's more, she didn't charge a cent for the information."

"You decided to meet with her then?"

"Not right away. I let her address sit on my coffee table for months. One morning after another tearful meeting with the Carrington girl's mother, I decided I couldn't face her again without something of significance to report, and I caved."

"What happened?" Addison asked.

"I drove out to the woman's house … well, if one could call it a house. From the outside it looked more like a shack until she opened the door and I went inside the place. I swear I'd traveled to another dimension. It was colorful and vibrant, and about three times bigger than it appeared on the outside."

"And the woman? What was she like?"

"Small and thin. Old. If I had to guess her age, I would guess she was in her mid-eighties back then. She was cooking a stew in the kitchen. She offered me a bowl and asked me to sit down. I still remember what that stew smelled like, the cinnamon, the basil and oregano, the whole bit. Best damn stew I've ever had. Guess you could say she turned out to be a lot different than I expected."

"What did you expect?"

He smacked a hand on his knee and laughed. "A gypsy with a crystal ball, I guess."

The waitress brought a second piece of pie and another round of hot chocolate. She set the pie in front of Briggs. He pushed it to the side and kept talking.

"She said she'd been expecting me, and she wondered why I

kept her information on my coffee table so long. I have to admit, I was impressed. I mean, how in the world did she know where I kept it?"

"What else did she say?" Addison asked.

"We ate together, and she asked if I'd brought a personal item with me, something belonging to Libby. The detective friend of mine told me I'd need it, so I had."

"What did you give her?"

"A scarf Libby crocheted about a week before her disappearance. I handed it over, and the woman closed her eyes, rubbed it inside her fingers, and mumbled a chant to herself. I tried to hear what she said, but she was too quiet. A couple of minutes went by. When her eyes opened, she handed the scarf back to me and said my journey would begin at the bottom of a lake not far from the city."

"Did she say where it would end?"

"She did not."

"Did she say anything else?" Addison asked.

"This is the screwy part. Before I left, she said she had offered me what I wanted, and in turn I needed do something for her. I thought maybe she wanted to charge me, so I whipped out my wallet and asked how much."

"Did she take your money?"

He shook his head. "This next part is why you interest me so much."

"What would any of it have to do with me?"

"The old crone said one day a woman would come into my life. She didn't say when or how, and she gave me no other details except to say the woman would ask me about one of my old cases, one I never solved. When she did, I was to relay the story I've just told you."

Addison pointed at herself. "You think I'm the woman she said you'd meet?"

"Has to be you, I reckon, and the woman's information was right. I found Libby's car at the bottom of a lake a few days later. Hoping to get even more from her, I returned to her house a second time. I arrived to find she'd gone."

"What do you mean, gone? Gone where?"

"Everything was gone. The woman. The house. All of it. It was like it never existed."

"What do you mean? How is that possible?"

He shrugged. "You tell me. I went back there half a dozen times. All I found was an empty patch of land where a house should have been. I couldn't make sense of it then, and I can't make sense of it now. But I believe for whatever reason, I needed to meet you before the case could be solved. So, tell me, Addison Lockhart. Who are you? Who are you *really*?"

CHAPTER 21

I'm not what she was," Addison said, "if that's what you're thinking."

Not the *exact* same, anyway.

"You can't expect me to believe you solve murders trained professionals can't just by doing a bit of research," Briggs said. "If you're not psychic, what are you?"

He seemed open to any answer Addison was willing to give. But sharing intimate details about herself wasn't going to happen, not with someone she'd just met, even if it meant she didn't get what she wanted. Still, she could offer something, a tidbit to keep him talking.

"I get feelings about things. If you asked me to put a label on it, I'd say they're premonitions. When I heed them, I'm often led to discoveries I wouldn't have found any other way."

He narrowed his eyes, considering what she'd just said. "See? You are psychic. Why do I get the feeling there's more you're not telling me?"

"It's like you said, we don't know each other yet."

He sighed. "I understand. You don't trust me. You can, you know. Your secrets, whatever they are, will remain with me."

Addison leaned back and folded her arms.

"Oh…kay," he said. "You're not going to say anything more, are you?"

"Not right now. If it means you don't want to share information with me, I understand."

"How about we make a deal?"

"What kind of deal?"

"Give me a day to think about it, and then I'll be in touch. I suppose it wouldn't be a big deal if I let you peruse an old file, under my supervision, of course. In the meantime, if you stumble across anything, and I do mean *anything*, I want to know. All right?"

If he'd known she had the evidence box, he hadn't mentioned it. She assumed he did not and stood. "I have to go. What you're asking is fair. I hope you decide to let me see the file. Thanks for the hot chocolate."

"Thank *you* for giving me a sliver of hope. It's more than I've had in a long time."

"Can I ask a couple more questions before I go?"

He nodded. "Shoot."

"Do you remember the address of the woman in the woods?"

"I don't see why it matters. It's like I said, the place is gone, and even if it was still there, she wouldn't be. She would have died by now."

"I'd still like to have it."

Briggs waved the waitress over and requested a pen. She pulled one out of her pocket and handed it to him. He scribbled an address on a napkin and offered it to Addison. "Might be a bit off on the exact number, but the street name's right."

"Thank you."

"What about your second question?"

"What was her name?"

He glanced out the window, tapping his memory. "I believe she said it was Joan. Yes, Joan is right. Joan Waterhouse."

CHAPTER 22

The history of witches had piqued Addison's interest from a young age. She'd even written papers about them in high school. The most famous Joan Waterhouse was the daughter of Agnes Waterhouse, a woman who had once gone by the name "Mother Waterhouse." Agnes had marked her place in history as the most famous witch to have ever lived, and she was the first to be hung in England in 1566 at the ripened age of sixty-three. She hadn't been burned, but death by hanging wasn't much better.

At Agnes' trial, she stood accused of killing her husband as well as one of the villagers by way of witchcraft, and though she feigned innocence until the day of her death, she admitted she owned a white-spotted black cat named Satan, and claimed he was her familiar. Satan, the cat, did her bidding in the unfortunate circumstance someone ruffled her alleged witchy feathers. Her daughter, Joan, was eighteen years old at the time of her mother's death. She stood accused of many of the same crimes, but Joan succeeded where her mother had failed and was found not guilty.

The name could have been a coincidence, but given Briggs' account of the psychic woman's house existing one day and vanishing the next, Addison wanted to believe there was a sliver of hope a witch existed who was alive and well. Since learning of her supernatural abilities, she had never met anyone like herself before, apart from her grandmother. It excited and worried her at the same time. Not having anyone who fully understood who she was had caused her to feel alone and isolated at times. Sure, she had Luke, Lia, and Amara Jane, but there was still a void that needed to be filled and no support group to fill it.

Sympathy was easy.

So was understanding.

Empathy?

Not so much.

Addison left Briggs and walked to the car. Sitting in the driver's seat, she stared down at the napkin in contemplation.

Briggs had made it clear Joan Waterhouse's home no longer existed.

But what if it did?

CHAPTER 23

Addison stared at the coordinates on the map displayed on her car's screen. It didn't seem right, causing her to wonder if she'd slipped up somehow. At present, she was surrounded by what seemed to be an endless field of garlic. She tapped on her GPS screen, which had frozen up less than half a mile from her destination point.

"Oh, come on," she said. "Don't do this to me. Not now. Not when I'm so close."

The way she saw it, she had two options.

The first was to abandon her quest altogether.

The second was to find the location on her own.

She'd come this far.

It was worth it to trek a bit farther.

Soon after, she came to a clearing, an area where the soil looked like it was being prepped to grow additional crop. There was nothing left to find. She let the car idle, leaned back in her seat, and sighed. She felt silly for thinking she'd find anything ... and defeated. The more digging she did, the more questions she had without answers. Since being contacted by Sara, the days had dragged on and on with no solution in sight. As much as she wanted to discover the truth, she missed the precious moments away from her family. She missed the time she hadn't been able to have with her newborn daughter. Luke had been far more patient than she deserved, and Addison suspected part of his reasons were selfish. He hoped his support would result in a faster resolution.

She didn't blame him.

Maybe they were both selfish for wanting their lives back.

Addison didn't care.

She sat back up, and her eyes came to rest on what appeared to be a cottage behind an old farmhouse. It wasn't what she imagined she'd find, but it was there, which was better than nothing.

She drove to the farmhouse and got out of the car. The warm, late-summer air drifted across her face, and she breathed in the aromas of vanilla and spice. Someone was cooking. The farmhouse door opened, and a woman stepped out.

Addison's heart raced, thumping much faster than usual.

She swallowed hard and stared back at the woman.

Could it be?

Was it possible?

Was it her, Joan Waterhouse?

The woman was younger than Briggs had suggested, and his visit had been decades earlier. If Joan *was* the daughter of Agnes Waterhouse, she would have been four hundred and seventy-three years old now.

"Can I help you?" the woman asked.

"I'm trying to locate a house that used to be around here in the early seventies."

"What did it look like?"

"A shack, I guess?"

"Hmm, I don't know," the woman said. "I've lived here fifteen years, and I've never seen one."

Addison pointed to the cottage behind the main house. "It may have been similar to what you have back there."

The woman looked to where Addison had pointed. "Oh, that's not old. It's an addition. I added it about five years ago so I could tend to my father before he passed away."

Addison nodded. "I see. You wouldn't happen to be Joan Waterhouse, would you?"

The woman shook her head. "My name's Rosalee. What's yours?"

"Addison."

"Well, Addison, I'm sorry I couldn't help you."

"Do you know anyone around here who could? Someone who's lived here for several decades?"

Rosalee tapped her foot on the ground, thinking. "There's a man named Horace Jenkins who owns a local produce stand nearby. He's lived here all his life. He might be able to help."

"Where can I find him?"

"Drive out of my place and chuck a right. He's about two minutes up the road on the left."

"Thanks for your help."

Addison headed out of the driveway and turned toward town. A woman dressed in a long, dark, hooded cloak stepped into the street. Addison gripped the steering wheel and slammed her foot down on the brake pedal. The car screeched to a stop.

Addison steadied her breath and grabbed the door handle. Before she could get the car door open, the woman vanished and reappeared in the seat next to Addison. The woman reached up and flicked the hood off her head, allowing her long, dark hair to cascade down her shoulders.

She smiled and said, "Hello, Addison. I've looked forward to meeting you for a long time."

CHAPTER 24

The woman was young, less than thirty, Addison guessed. Her skin was pale and white. Flawless. Still in shock, Addison fumbled over her words.

"Are … are you … Joan Waterhouse?" Addison asked.

"Of course, I am."

"And is your mother Agnes Waterhouse?"

"Bright girl. You know your history."

"I know my witches," Addison said.

"Is that what I am … a witch?"

"Aren't you?"

"I'm a lot of things."

"It's just, I didn't expect you to be so—"

"Young?"

"Well, yes," Addison said. "Briggs said you were much older. And, based on when you lived in history, you're—"

"People are funny creatures, you know. They see what they want to see, what they *need* to see when they need to see it. If Harry Briggs would have seen me as you see me now, he wouldn't have taken me seriously. It's an unfortunate truth, but it is one, nonetheless. Women aren't judged the same as men, even now, even after all this time."

"I'm here about Sara Belle and Libby Carrington. I'm trying to find out what happened to them, and I need your help."

"Of course, you do. You want me to wrap the details of their deaths in a pretty bow and give you answers you're tired of seeking because you yearn for your world to be perfect. You think you *need* it to be perfect to be happy."

"You're wrong. It's not true."

"I hope not. Put it out of your mind and make peace with it, because it won't ever be. You made a choice to use your abilities, to use the gifts you've been given. *That* is your life now."

"I came here because I thought you could help me."

"You came here because you're curious. You wanted to know if I was real, if someone outside of yourself exists in the same way and with the same abilities you do."

"Do you know what happened to Libby Carrington?" Addison asked.

"In a manner of speaking. I know she's trapped between the place she should be and the one in which she now rests."

"How can I help her? How can I help Sara Belle?"

Joan placed a hand over Addison's. Addison jerked it away.

"What are you doing?" Addison asked.

"Afraid of what might happen if we connect?" Joan shook her head and laughed. "Good. You should be."

Joan leaned back in the seat and rubbed her hands together. "You really *do* want to help them, don't you? I'm not used to such honorable intentions when it comes to your … well … the women in your family."

"I do my best to help those trapped in this world in any way I can. Briggs had honorable intentions, and you told him where to find Libby's car, but the car led nowhere, and then you disappeared. You could have given him more information, and yet you didn't."

"I had my reasons. What he failed to mention to you is that he hated his boss. He wanted to be promoted to his position. His boss was on his way out, so solving the case would have given him that, but it's not always best to have everything we want. Your agenda is twofold. You want all the lost souls who come into your life to find their way. You also want to protect your family, and yet you struggle with who you are and who you think you should be."

"Are you going to help me or not?"

"Stubborn, aren't you? This day is about much more than me helping you seek out the truth hidden around Belle Manor."

"Why is today so important?"

Joan stared out the car window at a flock of birds flying overhead. "Do you feel you know yourself, Addison? Do you know what you are? Do you know your roots? Do you know from whence you came?"

A sudden feeling of inadequacy washed over Addison. No matter the answer she gave, it wouldn't be right. "I know enough for now."

"I'm sure you think so. The truth is, you know nothing."

Addison crossed her arms, resisting the urge to go on the defensive. "If I know *nothing*, why don't you enlighten me?"

Joan narrowed her eyes. "Sometimes the veil between truths and lies is safer to hide behind. Once revealed, you can never go back to the way it was before. It's like opening a box and looking inside. You can't undo what's been done."

"I'd rather not spend my life hiding behind anything. I did that enough when my mother was alive."

Addison flashed to a younger time in her life when her mother refused to reveal her true identity.

"Take a breath, Addison," Joan said, "and then breathe out the pain you're feeling right now."

"What would you know about it?"

"I feel the weight you carry, the grudge you told yourself you'd shed years ago, but never did. You're still angry with her. Whether wrong or right, she had her reasons for doing what she did."

"I loved my mother."

"And I loved mine. It doesn't mean I approved of her actions—not all of them."

It felt like the conversation was flipping around in circles, going nowhere and everywhere at the same time.

"Why else did you come looking for me today?" Joan asked.

"You're right. I wanted to know if someone existed who's like me."

"Now that you know there is, do you feel better?"

"I don't know. Right now, I'm shaken up. I didn't expect to find anything when I drove here today."

"There are certain truths it's time you knew about yourself if you are to achieve your destiny."

"I'm not concerned about my destiny."

"Aren't you? Why do you help them then—all those lost souls with unresolved issues in the earthly world? You have a choice. You choose to get involved."

Addison shrugged. "It seems like the right thing to do, and I like helping them, most of the time."

"Much of what is known about my family isn't accurate. My mother was a shrewd woman, a woman most didn't understand. What people don't understand, they fear, and from that fear a false persona is born. For my mother, the persona became a label fixed to her chest, defining who she was, even though it wasn't. Most of it was for show."

"How was it a show?" Addison asked. "Are you saying she didn't do any of the things she was accused of doing?"

"You know what a *show* is, don't you? A production where one person tells themselves they're the star, when in reality, they're nothing of the kind."

Addison didn't follow.

There had been an abrupt shift in the conversation.

"You're leading up to something," Addison said.

Joan nodded. "Yes, I am. My mother was lynched, and I was

spared, but I wasn't the only one found innocent. My mother's sister, Sybil, was found innocent as well."

Addison was unfamiliar with Sybil, a woman she'd never come across in any of her historical research.

"I've never heard of her," Addison said. "Who is she?'

"My mother wasn't the most famous necromancer to have ever lived. She behaved the way she did to get the attention from the one who was, and yet, you won't find Sybil's name in any history book. She made sure it was left out."

"Why?"

"To protect herself, I suppose, and her legacy. To protect *you*, Addison."

"Me? Why?"

"You are her legacy."

"I'm … what?"

"Sybil was your, well, very great-grandmother."

"Is she still alive?"

"She exists, though she hasn't been seen in some time. After my mother died, Sybil left the village. She took her daughters with her, but left her sons."

"Why haven't I or anyone else ever heard of her until now? You could have found me years ago. Why haven't we met until now?"

"Like Sybil, I prefer to stay in the shadows, keeping an ear to the ground. I show myself when it's important. Today is more important than any other. Your grandmother died last year. I assume the book of enchantments is now in your possession."

Addison nodded. "I have it. Haven't been able to make much sense of it so far, beyond reading through the verses and trying out a few chants."

"You have no idea how powerful it is."

"I've only just started using it."

"I know. I felt the energy in this world shift when you uttered your first words from the book. You may know what's written in ink, but the ink is just the beginning. I'm here to tell you what else the book offers."

"I haven't found anything else, and I've been through it a few times."

"I have something for you."

Joan slipped a hand inside the pocket of her cloak, pulling out a shiny, red stone. It was small, no bigger than a kernel of corn, and circular in shape. She placed it in Addison's hand.

Addison brought it closer to her face and inspected it. "What is this? A ruby?"

"It's a red diamond, one of the rarest gems in the world. Less than thirty are known to exist. Do you know what a red diamond symbolizes?"

Addison shook her head.

"Red diamonds are made of pure carbon," Joan said. "They contain no impurities. They symbolize passion, power, and ritual, and most of all, the ability to be flexible in our form."

Addison thought of the red room at home. When Luke had asked what color she wanted it painted, she didn't hesitate. She knew it had to be red.

"What am I supposed to do with it?"

"Take a closer look at the book you've been given, at the women on the cover. Look at the center of the cauldron, at its shape, and you'll see where the stone is to be placed. Place it there, and then press your hand over it."

"What will happen when I do?"

Joan cracked a smile. "You'll see."

"Does this mean I'm a ... because you're a ... a witch?"

"Witch is a term I've never cared for much. We're necromancers. We harness magic and use it in whatever way we choose. You and I share the same bloodline. We're similar, but we're not the same. You communicate with the spirits of those who have passed on. I see into the earth, connect with its energy, see its secrets."

"You live forever, though. We don't."

Joan drummed her fingers along the car's dashboard. "You *didn't*. With this stone, you will change, your abilities will change. You have far more power now than I ever have. You just haven't tapped into it yet."

"Even so, if you can do what you say, you can help me find Libby."

"Don't underestimate yourself. You can find Libby. When you do, use what you've received from the book to the full extent of its power, but exercise caution when you do. You must be careful."

"Careful of …?"

"Have you ever wondered why the women in your family line are the only one anyone ever talks about?"

Addison shrugged. "I haven't thought about it much. When I learned who I was and what I could do, I assumed there had only been women because the abilities we have are passed down, grandmother to daughter to granddaughter."

"True. Males were born at one time, though. Earlier, I told you when Sybil left town, she took her girls and abandoned her sons. There was a reason for this. At the time, she believed the girls represented purity, all that is good in this world. The boys represented the evil and corruption that has plagued the world we've lived in since the beginning of time. Not that they were evil themselves. They weren't."

"You knew them. What were they?"

"Cunning, mischief-makers. I never saw them do anything I considered to be bad, but then, after their father died less than a year after their mother left, they left too. It is not known where they ended up afterward."

"Do any men in the family line still exist?"

"There are two. The youngest was born thirty-six years ago."

Thirty-six. Years. Ago.

It couldn't be.

What were the odds?

"I'm thirty-six."

Joan stared at Addison a moment. "Yes, you are. The boy is your mother's son, which makes him your brother. Your *twin* brother."

Her *twin* brother.

Addison wrapped her hands around the steering wheel, unable to speak. Every fiber of her being ached, her veins pulsing as the ugly truth filtered through her system. Thoughts raced through her mind like a horse sprinting free from the starting gate.

"Take your time," Joan said. "It's a lot to process."

For several minutes, Addison remained silent while Joan's revelation echoed inside her ears over and over again on a repetitive loop. She wanted to stall, to keep it from sinking in. She didn't want it to sink in. She wanted the last fifteen minutes in time to disappear, to evaporate and become nothing. It would be so much easier to pretend none of it was real. That *he* wasn't real. Because if he was, her history as she knew it today was being rewritten again—another version she'd known nothing about.

Somewhere inside, Addison knew Joan's words were true. She'd always felt a presence inside her she'd never understood before until today. It was clear now what Joan meant when she'd said the veil of truth was sometimes easier for people to hide behind. Addison had been lied to her entire life, robbed of the opportunity of having a sibling. And not just a sibling, a twin. A protector. It was the one wish she'd had for as long as she could remember—to have someone else like her in her life.

The truth was like a thief in the night, stripping her soul to its core.

It wasn't fair, and it wasn't right.

She wrapped her arms around herself, sucked in a lungful of air, and held it inside until she had no choice but to spew it all out.

"This is why you're here," Addison said. "To tell me about the red diamond, and my brother."

Joan nodded. "After the diamond came to be in my possession, I had a vision of you. It was many years ago. I knew we'd meet one day when the time was right, and I'd sit beside you and tell you what I just have. Everything in your life has led to this moment."

"But why? Why now? Where is my brother? And why was I never told about him?"

"I cannot give you those answers."

It was frustrating and impossible to accept.

Joan *had* the answers.

Why wouldn't she share them?

"What *can* you tell me?" Addison asked.

"Visit your father. The truth lies within him."

Her father?

She was angry.

Angry with him.

And even angrier with her mother.

How could they give up their own son?

"I know it will be hard for you to concentrate on anything but this, now that you know," Joan said. "Don't dwell in the past. Live in the present and focus on the task at hand. Finish the job you started, giving peace and eternal rest to those who seek you until you're sure about the calling which will soon be bestowed on you."

"You expect me to help Sara and Libby, and yet you've offered me no help."

"Haven't I? You didn't need it in the past, and you don't need it now. It's like I've said, *you* are the key to unraveling the mystery, Addison. And now that you know where you came from, remember who you are. Place the stone in its rightful place. Everything you need and everything you are will be within you."

She spoke of it as if today was a new beginning, a time to shed the past and begin anew—the same person she'd been, but better. She wanted to lash out, a place to put her anger, but Joan wasn't it.

"I know how I seem right now," Addison said. "I apologize. I'm not like this. It isn't me. As difficult as it is, I'm grateful to have met you and for all you've told me."

"It's been hundreds of years since I've shown myself to one of our descendants. You are far more unique than you know, more like Sybil than all who have come before her. Do not fear. You will always be protected. Be the strong woman I know you are. The woman we both know you are."

Joan peered out the car's windshield and frowned. "A storm is brewing, and I have places to be. Best for you to go."

"I'll always be grateful to you for today."

Joan nodded. "I want to leave you with a word of advice. You will wish to seek the raven, as the raven has scoured the earth in search of you."

"Who is the raven? What does he want from me?"

"Many things, but above all to make you like him. You must choose, Addison. You must decide who you will become from this moment forward."

"Why will I need to—"

Before she could finish the question, Joan was gone.

CHAPTER 25

Addison stood at the front door and steadied her nerves. For a small, fleeting moment, she considered turning around, instead of peeling back yet another layer of an unfamiliar onion. The curtains inside the house shifted to the side. A man pressed his face to the window and smiled.

The front door opened, and Addison said, "Hi, Dad."

"Hey, honey." He reached out, wrapped an arm around her, and kissed her on the forehead. "How are my two favorite girls?"

Addison glanced down at Amara Jane, fast asleep in her carrier. "We're doing fine."

He swished a hand toward the inside of the house and said, "Well, come on in."

Addison followed her father through the foyer and into the living room, and they both sat down.

"I'm glad you stopped by today," he said. "You wanna drink or anything? I have some juice in the fridge."

Addison shook her head.

Her father pointed at a power outlet on the wall. "I've plugged those plastic baby things into all of the outlets so she'll be safe to crawl around."

Addison mustered a grin. "She won't be crawling for a while yet."

He smiled at his granddaughter. "I'd like to hold her, but I'll wait until she wakes. She's such a wonderful, precious thing. Your mother would have loved being around for this."

Addison's wound had been salted.

"Dad, I need to talk to you about something," she said.

They locked eyes, and his smile dissipated. "You know, ever since you were a kid, I always knew when there was something weighing on your mind before you ever said a word. Same look you had when I saw you out on the front porch just now. Better to get it off your chest and come right out with it."

She considered how to frame what she was about to say, and whether it would be better to ease in or take a more direct approach. Her father had always been fair and kind. She had to believe there were only two reasons he'd keep such a big secret from her. Either her mother had convinced him to keep quiet, or he'd done it to protect her. Any other possibility didn't make sense.

"I need you to tell me about my brother," Addison said.

He leaned back, clenched his hands together, and bowed his head.

"Oh," he said. "Oh, wow. I hoped this day would never come. It's not because I wanted to keep you from the truth. I wanted to spare you the pain of it."

"What happened to my brother? Where is he?"

"I don't know."

"Why did you keep me and get rid of him, Dad? How could you give away your own son?"

"I didn't, sweetheart."

"I don't understand."

"Your brother ... well, the thing is, he is not my son."

"Yes, he is. He has to be. He's my twin."

"Addy ..."

His words trailed off, and the two of them sat there, staring at each other. Tears swelled in Addison's eyes as she contemplated his meaning.

"Dad? You *are* my dad, aren't you?"

"I mean, yes, you are my daughter, and I will always be your father. It doesn't matter how it happened. I raised you. I was there for you."

"*What* are you talking about?"

"There was someone else, someone before me. Another man. Let me explain. I met your mother right after you were born. It was a terrible, dark time in her life. She was in a lot of pain, and she was depressed. She wouldn't even eat—not much, anyway. Even in her grief, she lived for you, and somehow between the two of us, we pulled her from the darkness and gave her life again."

"But, you're *not* my father."

"Of course, I am. I don't have to be a blood relation to be a parent. I've loved you like you were mine from the moment I set eyes on you."

Addison wiped the tears from her eyes and stuttered the words, "Why didn't you tell me, before now? Why didn't either of you tell me?"

"I have always lived a life of honesty and truth. I never wanted to keep it from you. But your mother felt it was for the best, that if you found out she'd conceived you with someone else, and you had a brother, you'd go looking for them."

"I would. They're my family. Why did you go along with what she wanted?"

"She said if I told you the truth, it would put you in danger."

"Why?"

"I don't know."

Addison bolted off the sofa and slung the diaper bag over her shoulder. She wrapped a hand around the handle of the carrier. Her father reached out to stop her.

"Don't," Addison said. "I'm leaving. I don't know why I thought I could do this or handle this right now. I can't. It's too much. It's *all* too much."

Breathe, Addison.

Slow down and breathe.

"Please don't leave," he said. "I know it's hard, but there's more you need to know. You're right to be angry with me. Let's get it all out in the open, and if you need space to figure it all out, I'll give it to you. I'll give you all the time you need."

To keep her father from speaking the truth, her mother would have had to come up with a story compelling enough to convince him what she feared was right.

Addison released her grip on the carrier and lowered back down onto the couch. She threw her hands in the air and said, "All right, fine. No more lies. No more deception. I want to know everything."

He nodded. "I guess you want to know where your biological father and your brother are. I cannot tell you because I don't know."

"Are there any *other* siblings I don't know about?"

He shook his head. "No one else. I promise."

"Why wasn't I ever told about him?"

"I didn't even know about him at first. One night not long after you were born, we were sitting in bed, and your mother began talking about the man she was with before me. She said she'd become pregnant with twins and had a son and a daughter, which was you. I was in shock. I asked why the boy wasn't with her, and she said the truth about what happened with him was too painful to talk about. I dropped the subject, thinking one day when she'd moved past it, we'd revisit the subject. It took a long time for her to open up, and I still don't know all the details."

"What do you know?"

"The relationship with the other man ended right after she had you both. For whatever reason, they split you up. He took the boy, and she kept you."

Addison shook her head. "Mom wouldn't give her own child away and never see him again. It doesn't make sense."

Addison walked to the kitchen, and her father followed. She

grabbed a glass out of the cabinet, filled it with water, and downed it in one go.

"Listen to me," her dad said. "Everything your mom has ever done has been what she thought was best for you."

"How was giving up my brother—and not telling me—best for me?"

"Your mother wanted you to have a normal life, and she wanted a normal life, a life which didn't include magic. She wanted nothing to do with the abilities you have."

"How does all of this relate to my brother?"

"The man she was with before … he wasn't *just* a man, like I am. He wasn't, I don't know, ordinary, I guess you could say. Your mother said she was unaware of it until she became pregnant, and then he revealed himself to her."

"What was he?"

"I got the impression he had similar abilities to hers. When she spoke of the baby, it was with great emotion and sadness. I questioned her motives, sure, but I assumed she had a good reason to do what she did."

Amara Jane stirred in her carrier.

"I need to make her a bottle," Addison said.

He reached out, wrapping his hands around Addison's arms. "I'm sorry, honey. I am. I should have told you. How did you find out?"

Addison switched the kitchen faucet on. "It doesn't matter."

"Yes, it does. It changes everything."

He was right.

It did.

He turned and said, "I'll be right back."

Addison lifted Amara Jane out of her carrier. "It's all right, sweetheart. Mommy's here. Let's get you fed, okay?"

She stared at her daughter, wondering how anyone could let go of their child. And yet, people did for a variety of reasons. Although she couldn't imagine it herself, there were friends in her life who had, people she knew and respected who'd put their child up for adoption or had the child raised by another family member. In every instance, the only consideration was for the betterment of the child. Sacrifice was about being mature enough to make the hardest decision of all when it was the right decision to make.

Her father returned to the room with an envelope. He glanced at Addison, saw she had her hands full with Amara Jane, and tucked it inside her purse.

"What is that?" Addison asked.

"It's a letter from your mother," he said. "She wrote it right after you were born. She told me if anything ever happened to her, and you somehow learned about your brother, I was to give it to you."

CHAPTER 26

Addison sat across from Luke and Lia, staring at the letter resting on her lap.

"I … umm … don't know where to begin," Addison said. "So much has happened in the last twenty-four hours, I haven't even processed it all yet."

"Is this about Sara Belle?" Lia asked.

"In a way."

Addison relayed the recent events, starting with her meeting with Briggs and ending with the visit to her father's house hours earlier.

"Wait a minute," Lia said. "Your dad's not your real father? I can't believe it."

"I can't either," Luke said. "I never would have suspected."

"I've spent all these years thinking I looked like him," Addison said. "Crazy, right?"

"No matter what's happened, I know he loves you," Luke said. "Have you opened the letter yet?"

Addison shook her head. "I have no idea what to expect. He's a man I've called dad all my life who isn't my biological father, and I have a different father and a brother I've never met. I'm not sure I can handle any more surprises. I might implode."

"We're here with you," Lia said. "Whatever is in the letter, we'll get through it together."

"She's right," Luke said. "You're not alone, Addison, and you never will be."

"Thank you," Addison said. "I'm grateful for both of you."

Lia rubbed her hands together. "All right, well, we're ready when you are."

Addison unfolded the letter and read aloud.

Addison,

If you're reading this now, it means I am no longer with you. It also means you have been told of your brother, and of your other father, and there's a good chance you've become aware of who you are. It's true. You do have a brother. His name is Corbin. Right now, I imagine you're angry with me, and I expect you're hurting to such a degree I can only imagine. You think I kept him from you, and the truth is, I did. Not because I wanted to, but because making you aware of your father and your brother won't change the series of events from occurring the way they did. Please know every decision I have made was with the best of intentions. It has always been my utmost desire to protect you from the unknown, from things even I don't understand. I hope you find it in yourself to forgive your father, Bill, the one who raised you. He stayed silent out of honor and respect for me, even though he didn't agree with my decision.

Before I met Bill, I fell in what I thought was love with another man. Looking back now, I can't say what it was, or whether he tricked me into falling for him in order to further his own agenda, which was to produce an heir who would benefit from our combined abilities. His name was Sam, which I later learned was short for his real name, Samael. At first, I wasn't aware of who he was or of his intentions. I'd never met anyone apart from our own ancestors who possessed the abilities we have, you see. It came as a shock to learn not only were there others like us in the world, the circle once included men, too. Samael not only possessed similar abilities to ours, his seemed far more superior in some ways, like he'd had many more years to practice.

When I became pregnant, I learned of Samael's true nature. He showed me who he really was, a sorcerer who knew I was gifted, even though I had forsaken my powers and hadn't put them to use since I was a teenager. When I think on it now, I wonder if I made a horrible mistake when I turned away from my birthright. Maybe if I hadn't, I would have seen him for who he was before it was too late.

When Samael learned we were to have twins, he was elated. He assumed we'd marry and raise the children together. I had no such desire at the time. I was young and independent. I wasn't interested in being married then. I expressed this to him, inciting a wrath of anger and contempt. He wanted our children to be the most powerful entities to have ever lived. I wanted the opposite. I wanted the two of you to be normal children with normal lives.

I convinced myself everything would be all right, and when you and Corbin arrived, I assumed I could find a way to flee, to rid myself of Samael forever. To do this, I needed help. I couldn't stop him on my own. I was weak and out of practice. I decided my best option was to confide in your grandmother. I told her everything and begged for her help, knowing she would find a way out of my predicament. What followed is the reason you and she were estranged.

Your grandmother wanted me to play nice at first and wait out the pregnancy. Once the babies were born, she had a plan to save the three of us. She never told me her exact intentions; she just asked me to trust her. Several months later, the two of you were born. The day we arrived home, your grandmother said I looked tired and suggested I get some sleep. She offered to watch the two of you while I did. I woke a few hours later, finding you in your crib, but not your brother. I searched for him and discovered he was gone. While I slept, your grandmother made a deal with Samael. He could take the boy if he left the girl. He was to leave for good, and neither of them were to ever return again. I didn't want to believe it at first. I couldn't fathom how my own mother could betray me. But she did, and Samael got part of what he wanted, at least one child to raise the way he saw fit. He accepted the deal, and my sweet Corbin was gone forever.

I spent many years of my life in search of him after they disappeared, even though I always knew I'd never find him. I never did. Once they were gone, your grandmother had cast two protection spells using a book she referred to as the book of enchantments. One spell was to shield me from finding my son, and the second kept him and his father from finding the two of us.

I wish I could see you now to apologize. I'm sorry you had to find out this way, and I'm certain now that you know of their existence, you'll want to seek them out, to make them part of your life, as I did in the beginning. As you got older, I considered what might have happened had I found your brother. I have no idea how he was raised, who he is, or what he is capable of doing. There was good in his father, but there was also evil. Whichever road you choose to go down now, use caution. Think of yourself and of your own family, if you have one. And always remember how much I love you.

—All my love, Mom

Addison folded the letter in half and set it on the coffee table. She leaned forward, burying her head in her hands. Luke knelt beside her and draped a hand around her neck. He didn't speak, and neither did Lia. They waited, giving Addison the time she needed.

"Just when I think I know who I am, I realize I know nothing," Addison said.

"You know yourself, Addison," Luke said. "You know who you are—a caring, compassionate person. You're the same woman today that you were yesterday. The letter only adds more transparency."

"I have two different types of energy flowing through me, not one," Addison said. "Joan knew. She said I had to make a choice."

"What choice do you need to make?" Lia asked.

"When I place the stone into the book of enchantments, I believe I'll find out."

Addison leaned back. She stared at the clock on the wall, watched the seconds pass by.

Tick.

Tick.

Tick.

Moments gone.

Stolen moments.

Moments she'd never get back.

"I should be mad at Marjorie," Addison said, "but I'm not. I don't know whether my grandmother was right or wrong to do what she did. It's possible she knew who Samael was—who he *really* was. Maybe she was protecting us. I can't see her doing what she did otherwise. All I know is, I'm tired of everyone's protection. This is my life, and I can make my own decisions. I'll live my life on my own terms."

CHAPTER 27

Addison put Amara Jane to bed and went downstairs. She removed the book of enchantments off the shelf and held it in her hand.

I will uncover your secrets, all of them, the ones you've hidden from me. Soon enough.

She set it on the floor next to her and picked her cell phone out of her pocket.

Let's forget the old-fashioned way for now and bring necromancy into the current century, shall we?

She pulled up the internet on her phone and typed in the name Samael. She scrolled down the page. The articles she found were conflicting.

Some described him as good.

Others said he was evil.

Others still said he was a combination platter of the two.

Which is it then, Samael?

Are you good, are you evil?

Or are you both?

Samael was described as an archangel, an angel of the highest rank. Another article said he was the angel of darkness, one who brought about destruction, even though he had once been the chief of the warrior angels, the servants of the Lord.

Somewhere along the line, it appeared Samael may have been banished from the Lord's good graces. And though his kick out of heaven didn't mean he was altogether bad, it did lead to a fair amount of tomfoolery when he seduced Eve and impregnated her with Cain.

And here I was thinking Cain's conception was Adam's doing.

She was more confused about the truth of Samael's identity now than before.

And who had chosen her brother's name?

Her mother or Samael?

A secondary search of the name Corbin didn't suggest his name was anything of significance. It seemed to have neither angelic nor demonic influences. It was Anglo-Norman and was the average, run-of-the-mill name, with one exception.

The name Corbin signified a man with polished, dark hair and a brusque tone of voice, one who was also sometimes called a raven.

CHAPTER 28

"*You will seek the raven, as the raven has scoured the earth in search of you.*"

It had been among the last words spoken by Joan Waterhouse before she withdrew herself from Addison's presence. She'd said the raven sought Addison at night, with a desire to make her like him, whatever *he* was now. At least she hadn't said he desired to kill her or do her harm. Or maybe he did, and Joan had left that part out.

How did Corbin even know he had a sister, and how long had he known?

Maybe their father had told him.

Addison told herself it didn't matter. She had other more pressing issues to deal with, starting with an overdue meet-and-greet with Theodore Price, the sole survivor of the car crash.

Theodore Price's house was a modest, single-level, Cape Cod style, with a white exterior made of wood slats. Blue shutters trimmed the front windows. The yard was tidy and symmetrical, right down to a bi-level row of perfect, rectangular shrubs, looking like they'd been manicured by Edward Scissorhands himself.

Addison walked to the front door and knocked. A trim man with an absence of hair answered. He leaned against the side of the door and crossed his arms, staring at Addison like she'd interrupted his favorite television program. He was much different than the charming, attractive boy he'd been in his youth. And yet, his eyes were the same. They still had the same gentle glimmer they'd had in the car the day Addison had seen him.

"Can I help you?" he asked.

"I hope so," Addison said. "I'm looking for Theodore Price. Am I at the right house?"

He nodded. "Everyone calls me Theo. What can I do for you?"

"I'd like to talk to you about Scarlett Whittaker and Sara Belle."

Theo stepped back and waved a hand back and forth. "Nope, no thank you. I've relived that nightmare enough times. I'm done with it."

He attempted to swing the door closed, but Addison wedged her foot inside before he had the chance.

"Please," she said. "I have no interest in dredging up the past and making you relive it. I'm only looking for a few answers to just a few questions, and then I'll never bother you again."

He stared down at Addison's shoe, a knee-high black boot—a boot blocking him from immediate freedom. "Move your foot, lady. Okay?"

It wasn't the nicest response she'd ever heard.

It wasn't icy, either.

If anything, it was a plea for understanding, which played on an emotion she didn't want to have at the moment—guilt.

"If you could hear me out, I'd appreciate it," she said. "Five minutes."

"Why should I?"

"If you let me in, I'll explain."

He considered her request. "No. Now please leave."

His use of the word *please* furthered her guilt. She retracted her shoe and nodded.

"I understand how you must feel," she said, "and you don't know me, so why would you talk to me? I guess I'll figure it out another way."

He nodded. "Thank you for understanding."

The door closed, and as she turned, she heard the lock click. She bent down and sat on his front porch step, wishing she could reenact the scene, try again another way. A few minutes passed and she took out her cell phone, sending Briggs a text message:

You've had time to think.

Any chance you've decided I could take a look at the files today?

Two minutes later, he hadn't responded, and she decided to leave. Halfway back to the car the lock on Theo's door clicked again, and she turned.

Theo stepped outside. "What did you mean when you said you'd figure it out some other way? Figure *what* out?"

"I don't know … everything, I guess."

"What's *everything*?"

It was her chance, her one chance for a redo.

Where to begin?

"I want to know what really happened the day of the car accident. I want to know who the driver of the other car is, and why he fled the scene, leaving Scarlett and Sara to die, and you in critical condition. I want to know why the Belles became hermits in the wake of their daughter's death. A few years in hibernation? Yeah. Okay. It makes sense. Grief is a process. But decades? Seems like a long time to never get over it enough to live a decent life. I'd like to know why Cecilia Belle's mother Josephine was banned from visiting her daughter, until one day when they allowed her to come over, and then she died the day after that. I'd also like to know what happened to Libby Carrington."

"Wow," he said. "Anything else?"

"Yeah, one more thing. All these questions I have? I intend to find answers for every single one."

"Are you some newbie detective with nothing better to do than scour old case files? I don't know if they told you, but you're not the first one to try and reopen the case. You're not the second either. I mean, it's been a long time since anyone has, but do you get where I'm going with this?"

"No one ever gets anywhere."

"Right, and talking about it got old about twenty years ago."

"I'm not a detective," she said. "I don't work for a department, either, or a news agency."

"Then who are you?"

"Someone who knows more than they should sometimes."

"Ahh, well, you're going to need to fill in the blanks."

The door had already been closed on her once.

Why not take a risk?

"Have you ever had a dream you couldn't explain?" she asked.

He scratched his head. "I still don't follow."

"Have you ever dreamed about an event in your life or in the life of someone else and discovered something you didn't know— something you found out really happened? It may not have even been a dream. It could have been intuition. Let's say you knew you needed to call a friend one day, and when you did, you learned he was going through a depression because he'd just had an argument with his wife, which led to her saying she wanted a divorce."

She stared at the blank look on his face.

He hadn't.

She was losing him.

Again.

"I … uhh … no," he said. "Why?"

"I have those experiences sometimes."

He shrugged. "Why tell me?"

"I know a few things about all the mysterious events surrounding Belle Manor. Even though they happened long ago, I've seen them."

"You're saying you dreamed about something you couldn't know any other way, and it turned out to be true?"

"In a way, yes."

"Ahh, you know, I don't believe in those things. Not to take away from your own experience or anything. I just don't."

His eyes left hers and wandered back inside the house.

He was seeking a second escape.

"I have a pot roast in the oven," he said, "and my wife will be home in about twenty minutes. I should go. Good luck on your ... you know ... what you're trying to do."

He turned and walked inside the house.

Think, Addison.

Think fast.

"You were taking Sara to get ice cream the day she died," Addison said.

He glanced over his shoulder. "Yeah, I've told a lot of people the story."

"You wanted to take Scarlett to see a movie." Addison thought back to the conversation he'd had with Scarlett in the car. "*American Graffiti* was playing at the drive in. She said she couldn't go. She was staying the night at Belle Manor."

"Told a lot of people that too."

"Scarlett got upset with you because you offered Sara a second scoop of ice cream if you could steal Scarlett away to watch the movie."

He seemed intrigued now. Addison could tell. But it still wasn't enough.

"I'm sure you've talked to at least a few people about everything I just told you," she said, "but what about when you asked Scarlett what had gotten into her and told her she was acting kind of crazy? She apologized and said she had lost something, but she didn't tell you what she'd lost."

Theo staggered toward her. "How did you ...? How ...? There's no way. You couldn't know the rest of our conversation. No one knows I told her she was acting crazy."

"Theo," Addison said, "I think you should let me in."

CHAPTER 29

Given the meticulous, tidy exterior of the house, the inside made no sense. Theo, or his wife was—or they both were—hoarders. Hoarders of crystal figurines, hoarders of stacks upon stacks of newspapers, hoarders of an entire shelf full of empty cardboard paper towel holders. They were equal opportunity hoarders.

Theo followed Addison's eyes around the room and said, "The, uh, outside of our house is my domain. The inside is my wife's. For years, I've tried to help her get organized. I even hauled off a truck full of this stuff once. She has a hard time getting rid of things, so it didn't go over well. I blew up, and she almost left me over it. Now, I guess you could say I learn to deal with it the best way I can. That's love, I suppose."

He glanced down at his hands and avoided eye contact, like he was ashamed for her to see the conditions in which he lived.

"My father is like this to a degree," Addison said. "When my mother died, he refused to get rid of any of her things. All of it is still everywhere, displayed throughout his house like she could walk right back in the door and pick up where she left off, even though he lives somewhere else now—next to me, actually."

"You know why he does it, don't you?"

"I didn't for a long time. I do now. What she left behind … they're more than just things to him. They're memories, sentiments he's placed a value on, which makes them too precious to part from."

He stretched his arms out to the side. "As you can see, I understand."

I noticed an enticing aroma coming from the kitchen. "When you said you were cooking a pot roast, I have to admit, I thought it was a way to get rid of me."

He raised a brow. "I'm not a liar."

"I'm sorry for making false assumptions. I shouldn't have."

"It's all right."

For the first time since she'd arrived, Theo smiled.

"You seem nice. Come on, follow me to the kitchen," he said. "Why don't you tell me how you know about the conversation I had all those years ago with Scarlett?"

"It's hard to explain to someone who doesn't believe in things he can't explain."

"I'm sure it is. You're here. I haven't kicked you out yet. May as well give it a try."

Theo slid an oven mitt over his hand, opened the oven, and stabbed the roast with a prong.

"Yep, about fifteen minutes more, I'd say." He freed his hand and looked at Addison. "Go on. Sit down, start talking. Seems like you're good at it."

She lifted herself onto a barstool. "I see things sometimes."

"In your dreams?"

Close enough.

She nodded. "Call them visions. I have no control over what I see or when I see it."

"Are you saying you saw me in the car the day of the car crash? Impossible. Why would you even dream about an event so far in the past that has nothing to do with you?"

He may not have been a believer, but it didn't stop him from fishing for more information.

"The song "You're So Vain" was playing on the radio. You were wearing tan suede boots. You had one of them on the dash. I can keep going."

Theo was stunned. He slumped against the counter to keep from face-planting on the floor. Addison hopped off the barstool and rushed to his side.

"Are you okay? I didn't mean to—"

He caught his breath and said, "I'm fine. I'm just … well, in shock. Give me a minute to process."

He shuffled to the pantry, flipped on the light, and leaned over a shelf, pushing items to the side until he found what he was after— an unopened bottle of whisky.

He pulled it out and said, "I always said I was saving this for a special occasion. I suppose a shocking one will have to do. Care for a drink?"

"I'm fine. You go ahead."

"Oh, I will."

He twisted the top off and tipped the bottle back, taking a few hearty swigs. He set it on the counter without putting the lid back on and winked at Addison.

"Gonna keep this within reach," he said. "I may need another hit. I'm not sure my heart can take any more surprises. For now, let's say I believe you. What is it you want from me?"

"I know it's been a long time, but is there anything you can remember about the vehicle that hit you?"

"After the accident, I was angry. I ran it through my head so many times. I thought if I kept going back over it, I'd catch a glimpse of something I could pass on to police. I thought maybe I had seen something and blocked it from my mind because of how traumatic it was."

"And did you think of anything?"

He shook his head. "Sorry to disappoint. Scarlett was the love of my life, you know. I mean, the first love of my life."

"How long had she worked for the Belles?"

He looked to the side. "A few months. I can't remember the exact number. Most of the time, she went there on the weekend."

"And she was the nanny they hired after Libby Carrington, right?"

"When Libby went missing, the Belles laid low for a while. There was a lot of speculation about what happened, and from what Scarlett told me, some of the starlets who were regular guests weren't comfortable going there anymore. They didn't know what happened to the girl or why. It was a bit too scandalous, even for them, and they wanted to distance themselves from it. After some time went by and everything died down, the parties picked up again, and that's when Scarlett got the job."

"Scarlett wasn't worried about Libby not being found?"

"Worried? She took the job *because* of Libby."

"I don't follow."

"Scarlett wanted to …"

The front door opened, and his words trailed off.

"Dearest," a woman's voice called, "I'm home."

"In the kitchen," Theo said.

A slender woman dressed in fitness attire with long, gray hair twisted into a bun entered the room carrying a yoga mat under her arm. She brushed her lips across Theo's cheek and spun around, facing Addison.

"You didn't tell me we were having company tonight."

"He didn't know I was dropping by," Addison said. "I'm just headed out."

She stuck a hand out and said, "I don't believe we've met. I'm Harriet."

"Addison."

"Well, Addison, you'll have to forgive me for not cleaning up. The house usually doesn't look like this."

Theo and Addison exchanged glances.

"It's fine," Addison said. "Like I said, Theo didn't know I was coming."

"Why did you *drop by*, if you don't mind me asking?"

"To ask him a few questions about the car accident he had in college."

She nodded. "I'll wager a guess and say you didn't get far. He doesn't like to talk about it. Not even to me."

Theo stuck the oven mitt back on and pulled the roast out of the oven. "Dinner's ready. We'll have to pick our conversation up some other time, Addison. I'll walk you out."

They reached the front door, and Addison glanced back at Theo. "I'd like to ask one more question before I go."

"All right. I have time for one more question."

"You said Scarlett took the nanny position because of Libby. Why? Did they know each other?"

He nodded. "They were both on the college volleyball team and became close friends. Like everyone, when Libby disappeared, Scarlett was sure someone killed her. She decided to take the nanny position to see what she could find out. I didn't want her to do it, but Scarlett was headstrong. She wasn't the kind of girl who could be told what to do or what not to do."

"And did she learn anything while she worked there?"

"I'm not sure. She wasn't allowed upstairs, and she said every time she tried to look around, she was caught and had to find an excuse to explain herself."

"Who caught her?"

"The same person every time. Sara's father, Lawrence Belle."

CHAPTER 30

Briggs was standing in front of a bench, feeding corn to a flock of ducks when Addison arrived. The park he'd asked to meet at had a glassy lake in its center and was surrounded by sprawling, grassy hills. It was a picturesque spot to roll out a blanket, sip on a glass of wine, and look to the heavens, watching the sun's pastel colors ripple through the sky. Addison stood for a moment, taking in the display, the canvas before her serving as a subtle reminder of how much she missed when she didn't slow down enough to notice what was right in front of her.

Ever since Sara had appeared, Addison's life had been thrust into fast-forward, the disarray and unrest causing her to lose the power and control she once had. Plates may have been spinning, but she didn't need to spin with them. She needed to take them down, one by one, until they ceased to exist.

Briggs tossed a handful of corn and acknowledged Addison with a grin.

"Did you know you shouldn't feed bread to these feathered beauties?" he asked.

"I didn't," Addison said. "Why not?"

He sat down. "Several reasons. When uneaten pieces of bread accumulate in a pond, it can create algae blooms and deplete oxygen from the water. The term for it is hypoxia. On land, uneaten bread can grow bits of mold. When the ducks find it after it's been sitting for a while, if they eat it, they can get lung disease."

Addison sat down, thinking Briggs had missed his calling. Perhaps he should have been a teacher.

"Next time I feed ducks, I'll make sure to bring corn instead," she said.

"Doesn't just have to be corn. Oats, seeds, lettuce, duck pellets … they're all good."

In a conversation she'd had with Luke right before she left for the park, she made a promise to arrive home within the next hour. She had no time for chitchat.

"I visited Theo Price today," she said. "He's the guy who survived the car crash. The crash Scarlett and Sara were—"

"Yup, I don't need a reminder. I know who he is."

"Did you ever meet with him after the accident?"

"Of course. Visited him while he was in the hospital. He was in bad shape. I wondered if he'd ever walk again. Been a long time since I've seen him. How's he doing?"

"One of his legs still gives him trouble. He walks with a slight limp. Otherwise, he seems to be doing well. Did Theo ever tell you the reason Scarlett took the nanny job?

He nodded. "Not much I could do with the information. To my knowledge she never found anything of importance, and the Belles seemed shocked when I told them Scarlett and Libby knew each other."

"In truth, I believe she did find something—a locket, the same locket taken into evidence after the car accident. Cecilia Belle told me Libby was wearing the locket the last day she was seen. What I'm wondering is, how did it end up in Scarlett's car? She had to have found it at Belle Manor. Lawrence caught Scarlett milling around, and not long after, the car crash happened. Doesn't it seem coincidental?"

He raised a brow. "It does, but without a body, there's not much I can do."

"The car crash was no accident."

He stared at the shimmery colors the sun reflected off the lake. "Yup, I agree. Always assumed it was foul play."

After all these years, he seemed a bit defeated. What small shred of optimism he still clung to had become a pipe dream, one he no longer expected to come to fruition. He had lost hope, but Addison hadn't.

The truth was close.

She could feel it.

"Did you bring the file?" she asked.

He nodded. "Sure did."

He reached into his paper sack and scooped another handful of corn into his palm. The ever-growing audience of ducks steadied themselves, then scattered as he flung his hand in the air, showering them with one last feed.

He addressed the ducks saying, "Ladies and gentleman, the show is now over. You can all go home. Meet back here tomorrow, same time, same place."

He wiped his hands on his pant legs, reached for the file, and handed it over. "Don't get too excited. You know we found a minute amount of evidence. The file's rather thin."

"I was hoping I could borrow it, if you don't mind."

He frowned. "Not trying to be rude, but I'd rather you didn't. It's an old case, I know, and you're right to think I hold it too close to the vest. I spent more than a long time piecing together what little I could, and I—"

"You don't need to explain," Addison said, "I understand."

She flipped open the file, her eyes coming to rest on a small stack of photos at the top. She unfastened them from the paperclip they'd been secured with and held the first one in front of her. A dapper group of men and women were standing in front of a grand staircase, glamming it up in their Sunday best.

"Who are these people?" Addison asked.

Briggs lifted his glasses out of his shirt pocket, slipped them on, and leaned in to get a better look. "Okay, so, the last night Libby was seen, the Belles premiered a new movie, and they invited the cast along."

"What was the name of the movie?"

"*A Night in Rio.* Several cast members accepted the invitation along with a handful of Belle regulars. The people whose heads I circled in the photo attended the screening. Those I didn't circle did not."

Addison studied each face, scanning left to right. She looked for the man in the woods, the man who'd been chasing Libby. She was shocked to find he wasn't there."

"Did any cast members attend who are not pictured in this photo?" she asked.

He shook his head. "Not to my knowledge."

"You said the Belles also invited regulars. Who were they?"

Briggs thumbed through the pages in the file.

"I have a list. For the most part, those who weren't part of the movie cast were friends, and a few family members. Let me see … Here it is."

He removed the list from the stack and handed it to her.

"Big list," she said.

"The cast accounted for thirty-three of those invited, and the house guests added another fourteen."

"Forty-seven guests plus Lawrence and Cecilia Belle."

"They liked their soirees."

"Do you mind if I take a photo of the attendee list?"

"Don't see why not. Go right ahead."

Addison snapped a photo, slid the list back into place, and shifted her attention to a series of pictures of Libby's car being pulled from the lake. The car was dented, the onset of corrosion evident. It looked like a prop on a movie set—a prop that had been to hell and back.

"And there you have it," Briggs said. "The infamous car with no tales to tell."

"You didn't learn anything from it? Nothing at all?"

"Aside from the fact it had been submerged in water for months, even if there was evidence, it wasn't the same process back then. Maybe if it happened today, I would have had a better chance. Who knows? I was excited to find it. For the first time, I thought I was getting somewhere. It ended up being a huge disappointment and made the department look worse than it already did. People assumed we were incapable of solving the case. In ways, I suppose they were right."

"I'm sure the public knew you did everything you could."

"We were without a body or any decent clues. Libby existed one day and evaporated the next. My only option was to keep talking to those who saw her last until there was nothing more to say, and even that was disheartening."

"Because they all kept saying they didn't know anything?" Addison asked.

"The guests who attended the Belles' party were stiff and robotic. It was like a meeting had been called before we pulled them in, and they'd been handed a script, the same script, with the same lines to say. Sure, most of them didn't have a clue. But *all of them*? No way. Someone must have seen something."

Addison glanced at her phone, closed the file, and handed it back to him. "I promised my husband I'd be home soon, and I've already stayed too long."

"We're not done going through it yet."

She stood. "We'll have to finish later, if you're all right to meet again."

"Sure," he said. "I have time."

Briggs pushed the file into his tote bag and a photo slipped out, fluttering to the ground. Addison reached down and picked it up. Staring at it, she said, "What's this?"

Briggs leaned in. "Those two in the middle are the lead actor and actress in *A Night in Rio*."

"And the other two? The woman looks like Cecilia. Who's the man?"

"You're right; it is Cecilia. The man is Lawrence Belle."

"It can't be," Addison said.

"Can't be what?"

Addison held the photo closer, studying one of the men's faces. "I've met Lawrence Belle. This isn't him."

"Are you sure?"

"The man I met at the manor was my height. The guy in this photo is a lot taller."

"People do shrink with age."

"It's not just the height. It's his eyes. They're … I don't know … smaller. And his nose is more defined and pointy."

Addison thought back to her visit.

The man she'd met at the manor said multiple times he wasn't Lawrence Belle.

But Cecilia had said he was her husband—the night she'd visited the manor in her spirit animal form.

Addison had never seen his face that night, not all of it, but his voice was the same. She recognized it. She was certain.

"I've spoken to Lawrence Belle on several occasions," Briggs said. "And I can confirm, this is him."

If Briggs was right, if the man in the photo *was* Lawrence Belle, who the hell was living with Cecilia at Belle Manor?

CHAPTER 31

Ten minutes before midnight, Addison swallowed two tablets of ibuprofen and scolded herself for failing to stop at the drug store before she returned home to purchase something potent enough to assist with her persistent insomnia. But a pill wasn't what she needed. She needed something more—resolution.

To get it, she'd have to push a lot harder.

She headed upstairs, closed the door to the red room, and sat on a tufted, black velvet sofa from the 1920s that had once belonged to her grandmother. She crossed one leg over the other, pressed her hands together, and said, "Scarlett Whittaker, I invite you in."

Seconds went by.

Nothing happened.

She waited.

Still nothing.

She tried again.

"Scarlett Whittaker, I summon you. Come through the light. Show yourself."

After another minute passed, Addison received her first answer of the evening. It was just as she suspected. Her attempts to beckon Scarlett had been in vain because Scarlett wasn't in the earthly world anymore. She'd passed through to the light, and it was time for Sara to do the same.

"Sara Belle, I command you to appear," Addison said.

A bright orb appeared in the corner of the room, its shape bending and expanding until Sara stepped out. She rubbed her eyes, took in her surroundings, and stuck her hand up at Addison.

"Hi," Sara said.

"Would you like to go home?" Addison asked.

"To Mommy and Daddy?"

Addison shook her head. "No, sweetie. You need to leave here and move on."

"I can't. I don't know how."

"It's all right," Addison said. "I'll help you. I just need you to do two things for me first."

Sara huffed and shook her head. "No. I … I don't want to go."

"Why not?"

"I don't like being by myself. It's scary."

"You won't be alone this time. You'll see Scarlett, and your grandmother will be there."

Sara's eyes widened. "Grannie JoJo? She's there now?"

"Not yet, but she will be. She's been trying to find you so you can both go home."

Sara looked around. "Is she here? Where is she? Grannie JoJo?"

"She'll be here soon. I have to invite her to come here, and I will. I need you to answer a question for me first, okay?"

Sara pressed her face into Mr. Pickles' fur, speaking in a muffled voice.

"Sara, please look at me," Addison said. "I can't understand what you're saying. It's okay. You don't need to be afraid this time. No matter what you say, I won't be mad. You're not in trouble."

Sara lifted her head just enough for one of her eyes to peep out.

"I know what you want to ask," Sara said. "I know it was wrong, but I took it."

"What did you take? The locket?"

Sara nodded, her eyes still glued on Mr. Pickles.

"Can you tell me about it?" Addison asked.

"Do I have to tell?"

Addison nodded.

"Oh … kay," Sara said. "Mommy and Daddy were gone, and Scarlett wanted to play hide-and-seek. She said we could only play if we played upstairs, and I had to hide first. I hid under the bed, and she found me. It was her turn to hide, but she said she wanted me to hide three more times first. She started counting again, and I ran into one of the bathrooms and got inside the cabinet. I was in there a long time. I waited and waited, and she didn't come get me. I peeked out, and I called her name, and she still didn't come. I got tired of hiding. It wasn't fun, and I didn't want to play anymore."

"What did you do?"

"I got out of my hiding spot, and I heard Daddy in the hall. He forgot to take his money when he left, and he came back to get it. He found Scarlett, and he got angry."

"What did he say?"

"I don't know. He yelled at her, and she was sad. She said we were just playing a game and she guessed I was hiding upstairs cuz she couldn't find me anywhere else. But she lied. She *told* me to hide upstairs."

"What did your dad say when she told him you were playing a game?"

"He made her cry, and then she ran away. I thought I would get in trouble if he saw me, so I went downstairs real quick."

"Did you find Scarlett?"

She nodded. "She ran to her room, and went in the bathroom, and closed the door. She was still crying. I was going to knock on the door, and then her backpack fell off the bed, and the locket fell out. It was so pretty and shiny."

"What did you do with the locket after you took it?"

"I played with it for a minute. I poured it into one hand and then into the other one, and then I got bored and put it in my pocket. I was just going to keep it for a little bit. I was going to give it back. Promise."

Addison crossed the room and knelt in front of Sara. "It's okay. Thank you for telling me the truth. Did you open the locket?"

"Uh-huh. Nothing was inside."

"What happened after you put it in your pocket?"

"Scarlett came out of the bathroom. She said sorry for leaving me in the cupboard upstairs for so long. I asked her why she left me, and she said she got lost. I get lost upstairs sometimes, so I said it was okay. Then she went home."

"When did you see her again?"

"The next day, Mommy went somewhere, and Daddy's friends were coming over to play games, and he asked Scarlett to stay with me."

"Did she come over?"

Sara nodded. "Daddy wasn't mad anymore. He told her he was sorry, and she said it was okay. Grannie JoJo came over. She gave me Mr. Pickles and told Daddy she was taking me to get ice cream. She went to the car to wait for me, and then Scarlett and Theo got there."

"Why was Theo there if Scarlett was going to be taking care of you?"

"He used to come over and swim with us sometimes and Scarlett took him home. Daddy told Scarlett she was early. She didn't need to be there for two more hours, and he asked her to get some snacks for his friends for when they came over later because he was busy. I was going to get in Grannie JoJo's car, and then she said she couldn't take me for ice cream anymore, and Scarlett said she would. We left, and that's when … that's when …"

"It's okay, sweetie. I know what happened. You showed me. You just didn't show me everything, did you?"

"I … I can't remember."

Except Addison knew she could.

"Sara, I need to see what you didn't show me the first time. I know you don't want to, and I know it's scary. I'll be with you the entire time. Show me one more time, and you'll never have to think about it again."

Sara sat down on the floor, crossed her legs, and rested Mr. Pickles inside her lap. She squeezed his ears, rubbing them between her thumb and fingers. "I don't like thinking about it."

"If you want to be with Grannie JoJo, I need you to tell me everything."

"Promise?"

Sara seemed tormented. Addison could see it in her eyes. Going back into her memory the first time had opened an old wound, and the wound had festered. If Addison was to convince her to dive back in, she needed to go deeper.

"I had to remember something I didn't want to once when I was a little older than you," Addison said.

"Was it a bad thing?"

"It was."

"Did it make you sad?"

"It did."

"Did you get hurt?"

"My friend did," Addison said. "Her name was Natalie. We were in her back yard, and she was on a tree swing. She got too high, and she fell."

"Is she okay?"

Addison weighed the best way to answer the question. "She wasn't okay, but she is okay now. She's in the place you'll be going with Grannie JoJo."

Sara was quiet for a time.

Addison waited.

"Did you see Natalie fall?" Sara asked.

"I did. I tried not to think about it for a long time after. Then one day, I knew I needed to remember what happened so I could feel better again."

"Do you feel better?"

"I do, and you can too, Sara."

Sara's eyes filled with tears. Addison flushed with guilt, knowing she was about to put her through the traumatic event once more. There was no other choice. Not this time. Sara's inability to face the truth had kept her trapped in the void between one realm and the next. She was the key to unraveling everything, and she always had been. Addison knew that now.

Sara folded her arms around the bear and said, "Can Mr. Pickles come too?"

"Sure, he can."

"Okay. I'll do it, I guess."

Addison stood. "All right then. Stand next to me, and I'm going to reach for your hand. Whatever happens, don't worry. Hold my hand, and don't let go. I'll be with you. I will see what you see, and it will all be over."

CHAPTER 32

Addison and Sara were in the back seat of the car again. Scarlett and Theo were talking up front, arguing over the music, arguing over when to have date night. Scarlett said she'd lost something, and Addison looked at Sara, this time picking up on the shame spread across Sara's face over stealing the necklace.

It was different this time, knowing what was about to happen, watching the way Theo looked at Scarlett—like a million women could be in the room, and he'd still only see one.

Had Scarlett noticed his doting affection when she was alive?

And if she had, were the feelings reciprocated?

Scarlett gripped the steering wheel hard, like she wanted to bust it in half. She was a ball of nerves, a grenade set to go off. She wasn't just nervous, she was afraid. She'd found the necklace, and now racked her brain over where it had gone and how she'd lost it.

Addison believed Scarlett had found a secret hiding place upstairs.

It explained why Scarlett wanted Sara to hide.

She was buying time for herself to snoop around.

Addison wondered where the necklace had been found, who had hidden it, and why it had been kept as a memento, a token reminder of a heinous crime.

Sara's palm started to perspire. She clenched Addison's hand but didn't let go.

"We're almost there," Sara said.

Addison glanced out the window. The stop sign where the crash happened was up ahead. "I know. It's all right. Remember what I told you."

"Don't be scared."

Addison nodded.

Sara braced for impact.

The car slowed to a stop on what appeared to be a deserted four-way stop, at first. Knowing where to look, Addison leaned out the open window, watched, and waited.

She didn't wait long.

A black truck barreled through the stop, racing toward its target. The truck sideswiped the car, and Sara shot through the window, taking Addison with her. The truck stalled and then switched gears, preparing to take off, but it didn't, it idled. The driver thrust his head out his window, scanning the scene to ensure there were no survivors. He removed the mask covering his face, and his eyes fell on an image he hadn't expected, a tiny child blinking back at him, gasping as she took her final breath.

Then he did something Addison hadn't predicted.

He pounded his fists into the steering wheel and screamed.

"Sara! Sara, no! No! No! No! Oh, Sara. What have I done? What have I …"

This was his moment, his one chance to do the right thing, to rush over to Sara and scoop her up in his arms. Instead, he took the coward's way out. He thrust the truck into gear and barreled down the road.

Addison brushed a tear from her eye as she watched him. In the last second of her life, Sara had seen the killer, the man responsible for her death.

Addison planted a kiss on Sara's forehead. "It's okay, sweetie. I've seen what I needed to see. We can leave now. We can leave and never come back."

CHAPTER 33

Sara curled into a ball on the couch, sobbing. Addison hovered over her, wanting to remove her pain. Nothing she said would be enough. Not this time. Only one person could clear the salt from Sara's infectious wound.

Addison closed her eyes and said, "Josephine DuPont, I command you to appear."

Josephine materialized and rushed to her granddaughter's side. "Sara, honey, look at me."

Sara sniffled a few times and turned her head.

"There, there, dear," Josephine said. "I'm here now. Dry those eyes. Everything is all right."

"Grannie JoJo, is it really you?" Sara asked.

"It is me. I've waited to see you for a long time."

"I don't want to be here anymore."

"We don't have to stay. We can leave now, together."

"Where will we go?"

Josephine smiled. "To a beautiful place. You'll see."

Sara held up Mr. Pickles. "Can he come? He doesn't want to be left alone."

Josephine gave Sara's hand a squeeze and said, "Of course he can."

For a time, Josephine sat with Sara, and they talked as if no time had passed between them. When Sara settled enough for her grandmother to leave her side, Josephine said, "I need to talk to Addison for a minute before we go, okay?"

Sara nodded.

Addison and Josephine walked to the other side of the room.

"I know what happened," Addison whispered. "I know who caused the car crash."

"Don't tell me," she said. "Please."

"I thought you'd want to know."

"I've let it fester in me for years. Being reunited with my grandchild, I realize it doesn't matter to me anymore. What happened to Sara, what happened to me … the past doesn't dictate our future. I'd like to leave it all behind. I'm at peace with it."

Addison had never received such a request, and yet, she understood it. Josephine had been given a rare glimpse of the afterlife, into what mattered and what didn't, and it had changed her perspective.

"Of course," Addison said. "All you ever needed was to resolve it within yourself."

"I'd like to ask one last favor before we go, if I may," Josephine said. "If you see my daughter again, tell her how much I love her. Even if she doesn't believe you, I'd still like her to know."

"I will. Are you ready?"

Josephine glanced over her shoulder. "What do you think, kiddo? Should we get out of here for good?"

Sara joined Josephine and took her hand. A door in the center of the room burst open, shooting bright rays of light. Josephine's father appeared, beckoning them forward.

Josephine whispered in Sara's ear, "Do you see them? Do you see all those people in there? They're all here, waiting for you."

Sara clapped her hands and grinned. "Come on, Grannie JoJo. Let's go!"

They stepped through the doorway, and Josephine turned back. "

"I'll never forget you, Addison, and what you've done for me," she said. "What a tremendous gift you've been given."

CHAPTER 34

Two days had come and gone since Josephine and Sara crossed into the afterlife, and there was still work to be done, secrets to be untangled from the Belles' twisted web. But first, Addison decided to step back, taking a short sabbatical from it all to reconnect with her family and herself. The stone Joan had offered was still where she'd left it, sitting at the bottom of a glass on a shelf in the red room. At first, she left it there thinking she'd use it when the time seemed right. Now her head was clear. Now she knew it wasn't about a right time or a wrong one. It was about one thing and one thing only—the one thing she'd fought for years.

Fear.

Fear of what would happen when the stone was placed back where it belonged.

Fear of how it might change things.

Fear of the unknown.

What power did it hold?

What responsibility?

Unlocking the book's hidden secrets, if it *had* hidden secrets, was much more than discovering the hidden magic it contained. It was about unwrapping another layer of Addison's identity.

Two days ago, she hadn't been ready.

Today she was.

Addison stood in front of the shelf, peering at the stone inside the glass. It seemed pure and harmless, nothing more than a delicate ornament waiting to be fashioned inside an exquisite piece of jewelry. Now, it would achieve so much more.

She reached for the glass, tipping the stone into the palm of her hand.

What secrets do you have to reveal, and how will I change after you do?

She had a theory, a partial answer to her own question.

There was good in her. Most days she could feel it, the light flowing beneath her skin. It was radiant and alive, full of vibrancy and energy.

There was also something else, something hidden beneath the light. A veil of darkness was attached to the cracks and crevices of Addison's soul, to the few places the light failed to reach. The heaviness was something she'd felt ever since she was a child. She hadn't dared speak of it because she didn't know how. In the past, it had been something she herself couldn't explain.

Until now.

Her inner beast wanted out.

She could feel it.

Feel its longing to rise from its lightless chamber and become alive.

It felt dangerous and heavy, as if someone's hands were pressed against her chest, provoking her to anger.

Her mother's blood wasn't all that circulated within her. The blood of her father did too. And now she had to make a choice. She'd started to feel like a pawn in a much bigger game of tug of war, a game where everyone had an agenda, it seemed. Her grandmother. Her mother. Her father. Even Joan. The time had come for Addison to insert her own agenda, to fight for herself, for her own protection, and for the protection of her family.

Addison knelt in front of the book of enchantments, placing the stone where she believed it was meant to go. The cauldron sunk inside itself, molding around the stone until the stone was imbedded within it, and then the book ignited, filling the room with a brilliant ray of red.

Addison placed her hand in the book's center. A surge of energy flowed through her arm and into her body until her entire frame was alight. It lifted her off the ground, suspending her in midair. She raised her arm, staring through her translucent skin as centuries of knowledge passed down through generations of necromancers penetrated her mind.

She was no longer one.

She was all of them.

The glow began to fade, and Addison floated to the ground, coming to rest on the rug beneath her. Fatigued and drained, she rolled onto her side and surrendered to sleep. Some time later, she awakened to a faint, melodic whisper of someone calling her name. Her eyes opened, coming to rest on a freckled woman with long, scarlet-colored hair wearing a velvet, emerald, floor-length dress.

Addison pushed herself to a sitting position and said, "Who are you? What are you doing in my house?"

The woman smiled. "You know who I am, Addison. You invited me here."

"You're Sybil, aren't you? Sybil Waterhouse."

Sybil nodded.

"I didn't invite you," Addison said.

Sybil slipped a ring off her finger and walked over to Addison, sliding it onto her pinkie. The ring looked centuries old and was made of brass, with a red stone in the center. Addison glanced at the book's cover. The stone was gone.

"Is this stone the same one I just …" Addison began. "Did you …?"

Sybil reached for the book. The moment her hand touched it the book ceased to exist.

"What are you doing?" Addison asked. "Where has it gone? I need it."

Sybil shook her head. "You don't. Not anymore. *You are* the book, and the book is you. Can't you feel it, all the generations of your ancestors within you?"

She did feel different.

Changed.

Herself, but not herself at the same time.

"You are the woman you were before, but now you're elevated," Sybil said. "You can see and do things you only imagined doing before."

"Why is this happening? What do you want from me?"

Sybil turned a hand upward. "Nothing."

"You must. Everyone wants something from me. Why would you be any different?"

"It's not for me to say what you do with the gift I just bestowed upon you. It is for you to decide."

"Why me? Why now?"

Sybil crossed the room, trailing a finger across a few adornments on a shelf. She wrapped a hand around an empty bottle. "You know what this needs?"

Sybil pulled the empty bottle off the shelf, and it filled with wine. She turned her palm up, circling it in front of her, and a goblet appeared. She poured some wine into it and focused back on Addison.

"You look like me, and you act like me, except you seem a lot more uptight," Sybil said. "You worry too much."

Addison didn't agree but said nothing.

"You asked me what makes you different than everyone else, and why I chose to restore the stone after all this time," Sybil said. "My answer is simple—everything about you is different, and because you're worthy."

"Why didn't I know about the stone until now?"

"Some time ago, I gave it to Joan. Well, I didn't *give it* to her. I left it with her, knowing she would give it away again when the time was right."

"Why make Joan responsible? If it's yours, why not decide yourself?"

"I did that once. I allowed the book and the stone to pass from generation to generation until it was bestowed on Grace Sherwood. She was brought up right, but in the end, she decided to use the power she'd been given for her own personal gain. I stepped in and stripped her of it. Afterward, I had reservations about it going to one of my kin again. Joan has had it in her possession for almost three hundred years. She chose you because you're deserving of it. You are ready, Addison. You just need to believe it."

Addison walked to the sofa and sat down, burying her head in her hands. "This past week has been one revelation after the other. I don't know who I am anymore."

"Why? Because you discovered you have another father?"

"Samael is not just another father. He's a warlock, isn't he?"

"What if he is? Does it make him evil?"

"Doesn't it?" Addison asked.

"A warlock is a title. Samael is many things, and you would be wise to keep your distance, for now. Hone your newfound power before you decide to meet."

"Why?"

Sybil polished off her wine, flicked her hand, and the goblet vanished. "I want you to remove the idea of good and evil from your thoughts. You've sent worthy souls into the light, and because of it, the unworthy were cast into darkness. It was *you* who made those decisions, *you* who decided where they belonged, even if you didn't put them there."

"I have only directed worthy souls to the places they're meant to go."

"You did more than that. You kept the balance. You label yourself a good person because it's easier for you. It would be wiser to see yourself as you are."

"Who am I?"

"You're fate, the judge, the final decision. And so is your brother."

"My brother is the raven. Joan warned me about him."

"No, my dear. He's not. He's the son of the raven. He has his blood, as do you. Your given name, the one your father bestowed upon you, was Ravenna. Your mother changed it. Addison is a biblical name. It means 'of the earth.' It's derived from Adam, meaning 'life.'"

It should have been impossible to take in, impossible to accept, but somehow Sybil's words filled her with peace. Today, for the first time, the half she'd been missing all her life had become whole.

"How do I use the power I've been given?" Addison asked. "How will I know what to do?"

"Imagine what you want. See it. Manifest what you need, and it will be given to you." She walked to Addison and bent down, taking her hand. "You will achieve great things, and I will always be here if you need me, just like I was the other night at Belle Manor. Now, I must go, and I believe you have unfinished business which needs your attention. You are the judge and jury now, Addison, for all. Wield your power and be afraid no longer."

CHAPTER 35

Addison put Amara Jane down for her morning rest and found Luke in his office, searching the internet for a specific type of antique doorknob. After Sybil departed the night before, Addison had woken him and shared what happened. He'd been more accepting than she'd expected, making her willing to share even more.

"How's the search going?" Addison asked.

He spun around in his seat and sighed. "It's not. This restoration project I'm working on is tough. The Fordhams are hellbent on preserving as much of their house as they …"

Luke leaned forward, eyeing her.

Addison wiped at her face. "What's wrong? Do I have crumbs on my face or something? I just had a piece of toast."

"Your hair. It's a much brighter shade of red than it was yesterday."

"I hadn't noticed."

She stepped into the hall, walked toward a mirror on a wall on the opposite end, and leaned in, taking a good look at herself.

He was right.

Her hair was the same shade as Sybil's.

Luke walked up behind her. "Told you."

"Well, what do you think? Good change or bad change?"

He lifted a lock of her hair into his hand. "I like it."

"Good. I'd guess it's here to stay."

He stepped back, looking her over. "Wonder what else is different?"

"I'll show you." She turned one of her palms up and concentrated. A flame ignited over her hand. She swirled a finger in a circle until the shape of the flame altered, becoming a ball of fire.

Luke jumped back, his eyes fixated on what she'd created.

"Sybil said I no longer needed the book," Addison said. "This is why. I can do things like this just by thinking about it."

"What else are you capable of doing? Aren't you worried?"

Addison waved a hand back and forth in the air, and the flame disappeared. "I'm not. I'm … confident. More confident than I've ever been. It will take time to figure it all out. I don't want you to fear who I am now. I need you to see me the way you always have."

Luke nodded. "I do. And you're right, we'll both need time to adjust. I tried to remain calm last night when you told me. The truth is, I'm freaked out. I've become the skeptic, and you've become the optimist. We've reversed roles."

They locked eyes, and it was obvious. He wasn't looking at her the same way he always did. He looked nervous, like he was afraid what might happen if he touched her. She reached out to him, and he flinched.

"I'm sorry," he said. "Addison, I didn't mean to—"

"It's fine," Addison said. "I … uhh … I'm going to take a shower." She'd made it halfway down the hall when he called after her.

"Hey, what do you say we have a nice dinner together tonight?"

Seconds before, she'd been crushed by his behavior, but she could see he was trying his best. It was all she could ask of him. She glanced over her shoulder and smiled.

"It's a date. I'd love to have dinner with you."

CHAPTER 36

The gate on the road below Belle Manor was closed when Addison approached it. She flicked her finger in the air, and it came unhinged, blowing open. She grinned and drove on. She was met at the front door by the same man she'd met before. It was time for his identity reveal party.

He crossed the threshold to the outside, his arms stiff at his sides. "Oh no you don't. You're not coming in here. I'm calling the police."

He jammed a hand into his pocket, pulled out his cell phone, and shoved it in front of her face.

"Go ahead," Addison said. "Why don't we get Detective Harry Briggs? If you don't have his number, I'd be happy to give it to you."

"Who's Harry Briggs?"

"I get it," Addison said. "It's been a long time since you've seen him. Allow me to refresh your memory. Briggs is the guy who was investigating the disappearance, or should I say *murder*, of Libby Carrington. We've been chatting, working on reopening the case."

He swished a hand through the air. "Bull crap. I don't believe it. Why would he care after all this time? They didn't find her before, and they won't find her now. She took off, ran away. No one knows where she is."

"*Someone* knows."

They locked eyes, and Addison saw him for who he really was —a weak, old man.

She swept past him and entered the manor, surprised to find an older woman in the sitting room. The woman leaned back in an armchair, drinking a cup of tea. She appeared to be the same age as the man, and she was dressed in a pair of colorful, striped rayon slacks and a black blazer. Her short, gray hair was permed and somewhat covered by a scarf.

"You're not Cecilia," Addison said. "Who are you, and why are you in her house?"

The woman set the cup on the table next to her, crossed one leg over the other, and glanced at Addison. "Well now, maybe you ought to tell me who you are before you start ordering me around, eh?"

"All right, I'm Addison. And you are?"

The man stormed through the front door and slammed it behind him. He glared at the woman and said, "Don't you say a word. Not one word."

"You're not in charge of what I say or don't say," the woman said. "I'll do what I like."

The woman gestured at a chair to her right. "Sit down, Addison, and tell me what this is all about."

Addison faced the man. "You're not Lawrence Belle. Who are you? And why does Cecilia think you're her husband?"

"CeeCee isn't in her right mind, dear," the woman said. "Not anymore. She doesn't even remember who *she* is most days."

"Is it because of all the drugs she's taking?"

"The medications, you mean?" the woman said. "She needs them." "*All* of them?"

"She's not well, and to be honest, they make it so she doesn't remember."

"What kind of a life is that?" Addison asked. "She deserves better."

"Does she deserve to be in a psychiatric hospital?" the woman asked. "Because she'll end up in one if she goes off her meds."

Addison shifted her attention to the man. "Why did Lawrence plow into a car his own daughter was in? What kind of person murders his own child?"

The woman crossed her arms in front of her, her face ripe with emotion. "She was such a sweet girl, our Sara. The day she died was the worst day of our lives, one none of us will ever forget. You must understand, Lawrence wasn't innocent by any means, but when it comes to Sara, her death was an accident."

"Shut up, Flora!" the man said.

"I will not, Harold," she replied. "*You* shut up."

He shook his head. "Good hell, woman. How many weed gummies have you had today?"

"Two," Flora said, "and they seem to be kicking in. Hallelujah!"

Flora flashed a devilish grin at the man. It was clear she relished infuriating him. She seemed relieved, happy to share the family's secrets.

"Lawrence didn't know Sara was in the car the day of the accident," Addison said. "That much I know."

"He thought Sara was with her grandmother," Flora said. "He didn't know at the last minute Josephine had said she couldn't take Sara for ice cream, and Scarlett offered instead."

"I assume he asked Scarlett to run errands on purpose," Addison said. "But why did he want her dead? What did she find?"

"I don't know," Flora said. "If she found something, he didn't tell me."

Addison pulled the locket out of her pocket, dangling it between her fingers. "Was it over this?"

"I've never seen it before," Flora said. "Whose is it?"

The man swiped at the necklace. His fingers brushed across it, and he jerked them back, wincing in pain. "What the hell? Why is it so damned hot?"

Flora pressed a hand to her chest and roared with laughter.

"Who knew today would turn out to be such a fun," Flora said. "I must thank you, Addison. I haven't felt this good in ages."

Gripping his charred fingertips like he thought they would fall off, he scurried out of the room.

"What's with the necklace?" Flora asked.

"Let's just say it's temperamental. Who is Harold to you? And, are you related to Cecilia?"

"Harold is Cecilia's brother, and I'm his unfortunate wife."

"Where is Lawrence Belle?"

"He's … ahh … he hasn't been seen for a long time, not in the flesh."

"Has Harold been taking care of Cecilia all these years?"

"I suppose he helps out here and there. I'm her main caregiver. We've been close friends ever since we were kids, long before I dated her idiot brother. Worst mistake of my life, by the way."

"Dating him?"

"*Marrying* him. He thinks I use edibles because my back's in pain. I don't. My back's fine. I use it to get through the day with him. You know, his mother tried to tell me he was a bad apple, and I didn't listen."

"Josephine?"

"Yes, they weren't close."

"Why?"

"He never was the hard-working type. Hated work, in fact. Struggled to hold down a job, any job. It's why we never had kids. Couldn't afford them. He used to steal from Josephine all the time to pay for the lifestyle he wanted to have. Stole money, hawked her jewelry. If it was worth anything, he took it, until she cut him off and removed him from her life."

Josephine had never spoken of him.

Now Addison understood why.

"Lawrence killed Scarlett and Sara, but not Libby. Who did?"

Flora's gaze shifted from Addison to the hallway, and her eyes widened. Addison turned, finding herself staring down the barrel of a gun.

Hands shaking, Harold said, "Get out of this house. Go on. Git."

"Oh, Harold," Flora said. "Hells bells. Put the gun down, and stop being so dramatic. I won't cover for you again. Not this time."

"Get out!" Harold said. "I will put a bullet in ya."

Addison raised her hand in front of her. The gun flew out of Harold's hand, clanking on the ground behind him.

He stared at the gun, and then at Addison, backing himself against the wall. "How did you … how could you do what you just did without touching it? There's something *wrong* with you."

Addison walked toward him. "You're right, Harold. Something *is* wrong with me, and if you don't tell me what I need to know, I'll show you."

"No offense," Flora said, "but I think you already have. I'm either having an extra great trip today, or you have a magical hand, which doesn't seem logical, so I blame the weed. Trying a new strain this week."

Addison pointed at Harold. "*You* killed Libby Carrington. You chased her through the forest and forced her onto her knees. She thought you were going to rape her. You said you'd never forced anyone to have sex. You pulled out a flashlight, and right before you cracked it over her head, you told her she could scream all she wanted. It no longer mattered."

Harold slid down the wall until his body reached the ground. He wiped the sweat from his brow and said, "You couldn't know about our conversation. No one does, not all of it."

"Not even me," Flora said. "Not all those details, anyway. Is it true?"

"It is," Addison said.

Addison bent over Harold. "Why did you kill her? And where is her body?"

"It wasn't supposed to happen," he said. "Lawrence made me do it. He was always so private. He'd worked hard to keep parts of his life secret. I'd drunk too much that night. I didn't know we had an audience. We got caught. Lawrence was furious. And he ordered me to clean up the mess I made."

Flora clapped her hands. "Bravo, Harold. How does it feel to tell the truth for once in your life?"

"Lawrence didn't *make* you do anything," Addison said. "You had a choice. You *always* have a choice."

"I ... she shouldn't have been snooping around."

"What did she see, the two of you with other women? Was he afraid she'd tell your wife?"

"Afraid of little ole' me?" Flora said. "Oh, no, honey. You got it all wrong. I knew about the, uhh ... eye that wandered, let's say. Cecilia was the one who didn't have a clue, and I never had the heart to tell her. She can't handle things like I can."

"You knew your husband stepped out with other women sometimes?" Addison asked.

Harold glared at Flora. "Don't."

"Don't, what? Talk about your flirtations with other men?"

"What? Wait. Are you saying Lawrence and Harold were—"

"They weren't having sex when Libby wandered by and caught them. They were kissing, which was bad enough. You have to understand, it was a different time back then. It wasn't accepted. Lawrence was part of high society. If it got out, if Cecilia found out ... well, it would have changed everything."

A sound echoed from behind. Addison turned. Cecilia picked the gun off the floor and aimed it at Harold.

"You ... you ... bastard!" she screamed. "How could you, Lawrence?"

"I'm not Lawrence, CeeCee. I'm Harold, your brother."

Hands trembling, she tipped her head to the side. "No. You're lying. You're not Harold. You're Lawrence. You're my husband. My husband who betrayed me with my own brother!"

Addison considered removing the gun from Cecilia's hand, but didn't. Why offer Harold mercy when he had offered none to Libby?

Flora stood, moving in Cecilia's direction in a slow, somewhat apathetic way. "Now listen, CeeCee. You're holding a gun on your brother, Harold. Put it down now, okay? Actually, on second thought, don't. He's a murderer. He deserves what he gets. He deserves the life he's taken from us, the one we could have had until he ruined it all."

"You're right," Cecilia said. "He ruined our lives. They both did. I … I remember now."

Cecilia squeezed the trigger.

The bullet exploded out of the gun, piercing Harold's chest.

"Flora!" Harold shouted. "Look what you've done!"

Flora shuffled toward him and leaned over him, resting her hands on her hips. "What *I've* done? You deserve this, husband. A life for a life. We're all in this. Every single one of us aided and abetted in some way. We're all at fault here. Well, everyone except you, Addison. I'd like to point out, you *still* haven't told us who you are."

"I'm a necromancer."

Addison had uttered the words without thinking.

She waited for fear and regret to kick in, but it didn't.

Fear and regret was the old Addison.

The new Addison felt relief.

Relief that came from living her truth.

"A necro…*what*?" Flora asked.

"It doesn't matter. What does is my reason for being here—to see Sara, Scarlett, Libby, and Josephine get the justice they deserve."

Cecilia stared at Harold, the weight of what she'd done setting in, and she collapsed to the ground. The gun fell from her hand, clanking on the floor below. With what little strength Harold had left, he inched his body toward it.

Addison raised a hand, and the gun flew through the air, landing in her palm like a magnet. She released the remaining bullets from the chamber, tossed the gun to the side, and joined Flora, who was attempting to move Cecilia to the couch.

Addison hovered over Cecilia. She was still breathing. "She'll be all right. She needs a few minutes. I think she just passed out."

Flora stared down at her friend, her face filled with worry. "I feel awful. I shouldn't have pushed her just now. And I should have told her the truth long ago. Instead, we lived in the fantasy with her, going along with what she believed because it seemed easier. It may have been, but it wasn't right."

Addison and Flora moved Cecilia to the couch and sat down.

"Where is Lawrence, Flora?" Addison asked.

"I suppose if I'm coming clean about everyone else, I may as well come clean about my own actions. Several years after the car crash, CeeCee picked up the phone to make a call, and Lawrence was talking on a different phone in the other room. She overheard him tell Harold about the grief he still felt over what he'd done to his daughter. All those years, CeeCee and I were so stupid. We believed it was a random, hit-and-run driver who was too afraid to confess. What happened next ... well, it was awful, but truth be told, I've never felt sorry about it."

Harold moaned a weak, "Please, one of you call for an ambulance."

Addison and Flora glanced at him, and then Flora continued her story.

"CeeCee lost her mind when she found out what Lawrence had done. She stabbed him in the back one night while he slept. She thought she'd killed him, but she hadn't. She called me, and she was a frenzied mess. She said he was moaning and thrashing around. He kept trying to get up, but he couldn't. I went straight over."

"What did you do?"

Flora looked Addison in the eye. "I finished the job she started. Hard to say which one of us put the final nail in his coffin. Suppose we both did. I thought of Sara, of how much I missed her sweet face, how much I missed the CeeCee I knew when Sara was alive, and it was an easy decision. I was filled with rage, and ... well, rage changes a person."

"Where is his body?"

Flora tipped her head toward a jar sitting on the mantel over the fire. "He's in there."

"And where's Libby?"

"Beneath the addition that was built on the back of the manor."

It was why Addison had seen Libby in the window, and why Lawrence lingered around, roaming the halls at night, torturing a woman he once professed to love.

"After Lawrence was dead, CeeCee's mental state continued to decline," Flora said. "She started seeing things, believing Lawrence was still here in the house, believing Harold was Lawrence. She seemed to have forgotten all about what she'd done."

"I see now why you indulged her fantasy."

"Now you know my truth. Do what you want with it. I'm done lying."

Harold moaned a desperate, "Call 9-1-1. Please. The blood. I can't stop it. I need help."

Addison walked toward Harold, knowing what had to be done.

"We won't be calling for help," she said. "It's time for you to be shown where you're meant to go."

"Where? What do you mean?"

"One question, first. Why did you keep the necklace?"

"Why does it matter?"

"Tell me."

"I didn't keep it. I hid it inside a vent in the room I used to stay in upstairs. It seemed safe there, so I left it."

"Thank you."

Addison raised her hands in front of her. The wall burst into flames, opening a portal to a world Addison had never seen.

A terrified, flabbergasted Harold grabbed Addison by her pant leg, begging. "Please! What are you doing? Don't do this!"

The decision had been made.

"Harold DuPont, as judge and jury, I am the final decision of your fate," Addison said. "You robbed a young woman of an innocent life, and now you must atone. Go, and inhabit this world no more."

Hands engulfed in fire within the portal wrapped around Harold's neck, pulling him down as he writhed and wailed until there was nothing left of him. Then the portal closed, and the room returned to normal again.

Flora looked like she wanted to run, but she froze in place instead.

"You have nothing to fear from me," Addison said. "I know your secret, and now you know mine. I expect you to keep what you've seen here today to yourself."

"Umm, yeah … sure. Whatever you need."

"Good. Someone will be coming to exhume Libby's body. No one will ever know you or Cecilia had any knowledge of it being there."

"I'm not a good person," Flora said. "I don't deserve saving."

"What matters most is what's in your heart, and you have a good one. I can feel it."

Addison leaned over, whispering into Cecilia's ear. "Your mother loves you. Never forget."

She waved a hand over Cecilia's eyes, and they opened. Cecilia looked up at Flora and said, "What happened? Am I okay?"

A tearful Flora smiled and nodded. "Yes, you're okay, CeeCee. We both are."

CHAPTER 37

Addison stood inside the room where Libby had once been seen staring down at her through the window. The view outside was beautiful, the forest offering a serene feeling of calm, a perfect mask for the chaos saturating the walls of Belle Manor. The door slammed shut, and Addison spun around, canvassing the room, looking for *him*.

To the naked eye, it appeared no one was there.

She knew better.

Lawrence's presence spread through the air like an infectious disease, suffocating everything it touched. He pitied himself. He felt victimized, ejected from the lavish life he was meant to live. Trapped in the house since his death, his only recourse had been to vex Cecilia, haunting her until she'd gone mad.

"Lawrence Belle, show yourself," Addison said. "I command you to appear."

Menacing laughter permeated throughout the room.

The window rattled so hard Addison thought it would shatter. She raised a hand in front of her and released the hold he had, not just on the window, but on the manor itself.

A dark heaviness entered the room, and from it, Lawrence manifested.

"You shouldn't have come," he growled. "You shouldn't be here."

"You're a murderer, and I'm here to make it right. Today it ends. You'll no longer haunt Cecilia or torment Libby. You murdered your child, and I suspect you killed Josephine, too."

"Josephine was too involved for her own good. She wanted to separate Cecilia from me."

"So, you killed her."

"I did what had to be done. I never meant for Sara to die."

"I believe you. But it doesn't matter. If I would have known you back then, the man you were before the man you became, I would have told you to lead a life that made you happy instead of a facade. The issue isn't whether you loved a man or a woman. You led yourself to a dark place, a place you chose when you decided murder was a better solution than honesty. You deserved what Cecilia and Flora did to you."

He rushed toward Addison, his hands grappling for her neck, shocked when he failed to touch her skin. He turned his hands upward and stared at his palms, confused.

"You no longer have power, Lawrence. I have stripped it from you, and now it's time for you to go."

The portal split open, and Harold walked through, his charred body burning from the inside out. Lawrence backed away, shouting, "No! You can't take me! I won't go!"

Harold wrapped his hands around Lawrence's neck, engulfing him in flames until Lawrence burst apart.

The portal closed once more, and Addison stood there a moment, staring at the wall, hoping it would be a long time before the portal needed to be opened again, but knowing somehow it wouldn't.

"You can come in now, Libby," Addison said. "It's over."

Libby rounded the corner and stepped inside, facing Addison. "Thank you. Thank you for saving me."

"The one who you need to thank is Sara. Because of her, I'm

here. Lawrence and Harold have been dealt with, and I will make sure your family gets the closure they've waited so long to receive. Now, let's free you from this place."

Addison swirled her hand in a circle. A bright beam of light filled the room. When it settled, Scarlett was standing in its center. She ran to Libby, and they embraced.

"I always knew you'd find me," Libby said.

Scarlett stepped back, glancing at Addison. She nodded but said nothing, and she didn't need to—the expression on her face said it all. Scarlett held a hand out toward Libby. She took it. Together they entered the afterlife, and Addison smiled, satisfied her work here was done.

CHAPTER 38

"I know where Libby's body is buried," Addison said into the phone.

"You serious?" Briggs asked. "Where?"

"I'll tell you, under one condition. Cecilia Belle has been through a lot in her life. So has her sister-in-law, Flora DuPont. They don't need to be put through anything else when word gets out."

"I'll do everything I can to make sure they're far from the noise these types of situations cause. Believe me, I understand what scrutiny is like. You can trust me. I give you my word."

Trust.

It was a fickle, fleeting thing.

Still, she'd offer Libby's location, allowing him a chance to earn the trust she was about to bestow on him. She outlined the story for Briggs in a way that freed Cecilia and Flora from any wrongdoing. Libby was buried beneath the addition to the house. She'd been murdered by Harold, who'd been pressured by Lawrence to take care of the situation when they'd been caught.

Then Scarlett came snooping around. She'd been caught with Libby's necklace. Lawrence decided she needed to be dealt with and had sent her on a specific errand, which placed her at a quiet intersection where he wouldn't have trouble making his getaway once the deed was done. He'd only mistook one thing—he didn't know his daughter would be in the car.

Briggs had more questions than answers Addison couldn't give them if she wanted to spare Cecilia and Flora from being charged as accessories to murder, or with murder themselves.

"Are you trying to tell me neither one of their wives had any idea what went on?" he asked.

"I'm asking you to leave them out of it. Whether they knew or they didn't, what Harold and Lawrence did wasn't their fault. They had no part in the murders."

"That's one hell of a condition."

"It's been decades, Briggs. Give Scarlett and Libby's families closure and let that be the end of it."

"How do you know all this?" he asked.

"It's better if I don't say."

"Better for you?"

"This isn't about me. I'm not thinking of myself here."

"What about Lawrence and Harold? Where can I find those two bastards?"

"They're gone. Lawrence hasn't lived at the manor for many years. Flora DuPont has been taking care of Cecilia all this time."

"How am I supposed to—"

"Do you believe in karma, Briggs?" Addison asked.

"I'd like to think it exists. S'pose I don't, though."

"I do, and I believe Harold and Lawrence got what they deserved."

"Think so? Guess you won't elaborate on that, either."

He was right.

Best she didn't.

CHAPTER 39

One of Addison's fondest memories was a trip she'd taken with her father after she graduated from high school. She'd spent four years learning Spanish, and he'd rewarded her hard work with a surprise trip to Spain. They rented a villa overlooking the ocean, and she'd wake early each morning, wrap a blanket around her, and sit outside, waiting for the sun to rise.

For years, she'd wanted to go back and hadn't.

Not until today.

When his name left her lips and she invited him in, she felt a sense of unity, confirmation that her decision to make contact was right. In the distance, a man dressed in black walked toward her. She stood, brushed the sand off the bottom of her dress, and clasped her hands together, waiting.

He reached her, and a smile spread across his face.

"I thought this day would never come," he said. "I can't believe I'm here, looking at you. It doesn't seem real."

"It is."

Corbin was tall and slender, with dark hair and piercing blue eyes the shade of a robin's egg. There was a kindness about him. She could feel it. But he was also shrouded in mystery.

He turned his head and stared out into the ocean. "This place, it's beautiful. Where are we?"

"I decided it would be good if we met somewhere neutral for the first time. I imagined one of my favorite places, and here we are."

"Can I …? Is it all right to touch you, to give you a hug?"

She nodded.

He pulled her close, and they embraced.

"I've thought about you my entire life," he said. "I tried to imagine what you looked like, what kind of person you turned out to be. All I have ever wanted was to find you."

"I didn't know you existed until a few days ago. But then, there are a lot of things I didn't know until a few days ago. I thought my dad, the one who raised me, was my real father."

"Is he a good man, the one who raised you?"

"He's great."

"Then, in many ways, he's still your father."

He was right, and when she returned home, she'd make things good again.

"Did your father, or I guess I should say *our* father, tell you about me?" she asked. "Did he tell you about our mother?"

He nodded. "I've heard stories about their relationship, and I know what happened in the end. He told me about the deal Marjorie made with him. He loved her, you know, our mother?"

"I think she thought he used her to create us—a special breed, so to speak."

"It was complicated. He wanted us all to be together, to raise us with the full use of the power we possess. He thought he could sway her to see things his way, but she hated magic. He never wanted to leave you. It was a hard decision."

"He still made it."

Corbin's expression was one of empathy.

She wasn't the only one who had missed out—he had, too.

"Tell me about your life," he said. "What was it like?"

"I knew I was different than other kids as a child, but it was something I didn't understand. My mother never relented on her decision to keep magic out of my life, and for a long time, it was dormant. Several years ago, she was in a car accident and died. I inherited our family's manor, a manor I hadn't known about before her death, and the moment I stepped foot inside of it, everything changed. I've been learning more and more about who I am ever since."

"She's ... dead?"

"I'm sorry. I'm sure you hoped you would be able to connect with her now, but you should know she never forgot about you."

"I wish I could have met her."

"What's our father like?" Addison asked.

"He is many things. Determined. Headstrong. He is a good father, but he has many expectations, and sometimes in his haste to achieve what he wants, and what he believes is important, he doesn't think things through."

"In what way?"

Corbin pushed his hands inside his pockets, thinking. "Let's talk more about him another time. Right now, I want to focus on you. What do you do with the power you possess?"

"Lost souls come to me, those trapped here on earth after they have died because of an event that kept them from moving on. I help them find their way. I send them into the afterlife."

"Always to heaven, never to hell?"

"Why do you ask?"

"I felt something today, earlier, before you called my name. You opened the portal."

She fiddled with the ring on her finger. "I made a decision I've never had to make before, one I never knew I *could* make until now."

He stared at her hand. "It makes sense. You have the stone."

"Sybil gave it to me. How do you know about it?"

"Our father has been around for centuries. He's known Sybil

for ages. I know of the ring's significance. It's been out of play for a long time. It holds more power than you know."

Oh, she knew.

"I have no interest in power for myself."

"You misunderstand me. The ring itself *is* power. It's all the energy of the universe combined. My father said if it was ever passed to one of Sybil's descendants again, the bearer of the stone would rule on behalf of both worlds."

"Are we talking heaven and hell, or …?"

"I don't know."

"I have no interest in ruling over anything. I opened the portal to send two men where they deserved to go."

He nodded. "Don't you see? You could do so much more. You could place judgment on entire countries if you wanted."

She did see.

She saw her father's influence.

It was why she'd been given the ring, why Joan and Sybil put their faith in her.

She assumed her father would relish the idea of a daughter who had the ultimate gift bestowed upon her. If so, if they ever crossed paths, he would be disappointed. He'd never get the daughter he'd always wanted.

"You give life and you take it," Corbin said. "I just take it. I seek out those who waste their lives, achieving nothing. They're not good or bad. They're satisfied in being no one. Their indifference tells me they don't belong here, that the world is better once they're erased."

"You choose *for* them? What if what you see as indifference today changes tomorrow?"

"It won't change tomorrow, or any other day for the rest of their life."

"How can you be so sure?"

"I see inside their hearts, as you now do with those you seek. For some, change isn't possible."

Addison shook her head. "I shouldn't feel sorry for them, I guess, but I do."

He smiled. "You really are as good as I thought you to be. I admire you for it."

"I won't serve our father's agenda."

"I understand."

But would their father?

Would he understand?

Addison glanced at the time and thought of Luke. "I need to go, Corbin."

"Please, can't you stay a bit longer?"

"I can't. Not today."

"Can I see you again? I want to be part of your life."

Addison reached out and took his hand in hers, feeling a rush of energy flow between them. "You will see me again. I'll call on you once I've settled into the new role I've been given. I have much to learn."

"I look forward to seeing you again, Addison."

She took his hands in hers, holding them until he faded from sight, and then she remained there a moment, pressing her toes into the fine grains of sand, pondering life, and the changes yet to come. She'd been given a great responsibility, which would have seemed too much to bear a couple of short weeks earlier.

Now she was certain.

Life would go on and she would adapt.

She was ready.

She just had an important dinner date to get to first.

***

Thank you for reading BELLE MANOR HAUNTING, book four in the Addison Lockhart ghost mystery series.

When I started this series, I planned to make it a trilogy and end it there, but as Addison's character has developed over the years, I found there was so much more I wanted to do with her. In the book you just read, Addison's life takes several twists and turns, and she finally realizes who she is and who she's been all along. We'll explore her new abilities a lot more in book 5.

ABOUT CHERYL BRADSHAW

Cheryl Bradshaw is a *New York Times* and *USA Today* bestselling author writing in the genres of mystery, thriller, paranormal suspense, and romantic suspense, among others. Her novel *Stranger in Town* (Sloane Monroe series #4) was a 2013 Shamus Award finalist for Best PI Novel of the Year, and her novel *I Have a Secret* (Sloane Monroe series #3) was a 2013 eFestival of Words winner for Best Thriller. To date, nine of Cheryl's novels have made the *USA Today* bestselling books list.

Books by Cheryl Bradshaw

Sloane Monroe Series

Black Diamond Death (Book 1)
Charlotte Halliwell has a secret. But before revealing it to her sister, she's found dead.

Murder in Mind (Book 2)
A woman is found murdered, the serial killer's trademark "S" carved into her wrist.

I Have a Secret (Book 3)
Doug Ward has been running from his past for twenty years. But after his fourth whisky of the night, he doesn't want to keep quiet, not anymore.

Stranger in Town (Book 4)

A frantic mother runs down the aisles, searching for her missing daughter. But little Olivia is already gone.

Bed of Bones (Book 5)

Sometimes even the deepest, darkest secrets find their way to the surface.

Flirting with Danger (Book 5.5) A Sloane Monroe Short Story

A fancy hotel. A weekend getaway. For Sloane Monroe, rest has finally arrived, until the lights go out, a woman screams, and Sloane's nightmare begins.

Hush Now Baby (Book 6)

Serena Westwood tiptoes to her baby's crib and looks inside, startled to find her newborn son is gone.

Dead of Night (Book 6.5) A Sloane Monroe Short Story

After her mother-in-law is fatally stabbed, Wren is seen fleeing with the bloody knife. Is Wren the killer, or is a dark, scandalous family secret to blame?

Gone Daddy Gone (Book 7)

A man lurks behind Shelby in the park. Who is he? And why does he have a gun?

Smoke & Mirrors (Book 8)

Grace Ashby wakes to the sound of a horrifying scream. She races down the hallway, finding her mother's lifeless body on the floor in a pool of blood. Her mother's boyfriend Hugh is hunched over her, but is Hugh really her mother's killer?

Sloane Monroe Stories: Deadly Sins

Deadly Sins: Sloth (Book 1)
Darryl has been shot, and a mysterious woman is sprawled out on the floor in his hallway. She's dead too. Who is she? And why have they both been murdered?

Deadly Sins: Wrath (Book 2)
Headlights flash through Maddie's car's back windshield, someone following close behind. When her car careens into a nearby tree, the chase comes to an end. But for Maddie, the end is just the beginning.

Deadly Sins: Lust (Book 3)
Marissa Calhoun sits alone on a beach-like swimming hole nestled on Australia's foreshore. Tonight the lagoon is hers and hers alone. Or is it?

Deadly Sins: Greed (Book 4)
It was just another day for mob boss Giovanni Luciana until he took his car for a drive.

Addison Lockhart Series

Grayson Manor Haunting (Book 1)
When Addison Lockhart inherits Grayson Manor after her mother's untimely death, she unlocks a secret that's been kept hidden for over fifty years.

Rosecliff Manor Haunting (Book 2)
Addison Lockhart jolts awake. The dream had seemed so real. Eleven-year-old twins Vivian and Grace were so full of life, but they couldn't be. They've been dead for over forty years.

Blackthorn Manor Haunting (Book 3)

Addison Lockhart leans over the manor's window, gasping when she feels a hand on her back. She grabs the windowsill to brace herself, but it's too late--she's already falling.

Belle Manor Haunting (Book 4)

A vehicle barrels through the stop sign, slamming into the car Addison Lockhart is inside before fleeing the scene. Who is the driver of the other car? And what secrets within the walls of Belle Manor will provide the answer?

TILL DEATH DO US PART NOVELLA SERIES

Whispers of Murder (Book 1)

It was Isabelle Donnelly's wedding day, a moment in time that should have been the happiest in her life...until it ended in murder.

Echoes of Murder (Book 2)

When two women are found dead at the same wedding, medical examiner Reagan Davenport will stop at nothing to discover the identity of the killer.

STAND-ALONE NOVELS

Eye for Revenge

Quinn Montgomery wakes to find herself in the hospital. Her childhood best friend Evie is dead, and Evie's four-year-old son witnessed it all. Traumatized over what he saw, he hasn't spoken.

The Perfect Lie
When true-crime writer Alexandria Weston is found murdered on the last stop of her book tour, fellow writer Joss Jax steps in to investigate.

Hickory Dickory Dead
Maisie Fezziwig wakes to a harrowing scream outside. Curious, she walks outside to investigate, and Maisie stumbles on a grisly murder that will change her life forever.

Roadkill
Suburban housewife Juliette Granger has been living a secret life ... a life that's about to turn deadly for everyone she loves.